Angel of Mercy
In a time of jazz and bathtub gin, death stalks New Orleans.
Captain Mooney must root out the cause.

The Green Knight
What if old myths and legends carry a grain of truth?
When he discovers this, Gavin Baddock must keep his head.

Oppositional
A loving wife, a mysterious patron, and dark secrets.
Will Phillip DeGranz fall prey to his desire for knowledge?

Cupids
Sometimes you get more than you bargained for.
An old collector. A private moon. A cherub run amok.

To Catch a Thief
Sheriff Larry Crabtree's quiet community hides a dark secret.
Larry must unlearn his common sense and rational ways.

Malaya

How well do we ever know our spouses?
Sometimes secrets shared mean secrets kept.

Swift's

Take a short look into a world of short ribs.
And don't question the source.

Birth of the Makmorn

Two elders face a menace from before the time of
stories.
Can strength and loyalty prevail against primordial
hate?

JASON A. ADAMS

Tales From the Squirrel Garden

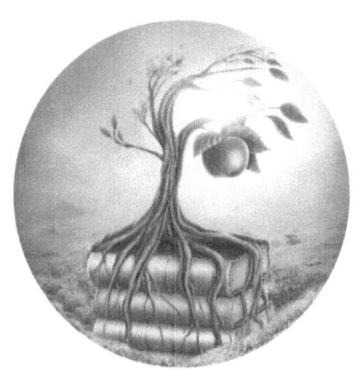

Spiral Publishing, Ltd.

Tales from the Squirrel Garden: Volume 1

Published 2020 by Spiral Publishing, Ltd. www.spiralpublishing.net

Book and cover design copyright © 2020 by Spiral Publishing, Ltd.

Cover art copyright © 2020 by egal/Dreamstime

ISBN-13: 978-1-948890-49-6
Large Print ISBN-13: 978-1-948890-50-2
Hardcover ISBN-13: 978-1-63992-065-5

Library of Congress Control Number: 2020932861

*To all the great tale-spinners whose short stories
have been and continue to be an inspiration.*

CONTENTS

INTRODUCTION

Greetings, O Reader, and welcome to my world!

Tales From the Squirrel Garden: Volume 1 is the first collection of my short fiction, but certainly not the last. Inside you'll find several stories across a range of genres. Some are darker than others, some a little more light-hearted.

I hope you find all of them entertaining.

And that you have interesting dreams tonight.

Angel of Mercy takes you back to the New Orleans of the early 20th Century, following the trail of a serial killer alongside an intrepid police captain. This was my first foray into period fiction, and was a lot of fun to write. I'm a huge history buff, and almost got so caught up in the research I forgot to actually write the story.

What if the old myths and legends have a kernel of truth? *The Green Knight* tries to answer the question. Set in modern Atlanta, this one asks the difficult questions through the eyes of a hapless ambulance-chasing lawyer who learns more than he expected.

Sometimes writers have to take a good long look at themselves and ask where this stuff comes from. *Oppositional* is a story I started on a wonderful trip to Romania. I deliberately tried to capture the feel of a Victorian horror story, hopefully with some success. While I had fun with the writing, this is a story that makes some of my loved ones give me That Look.

Cupids came from a Science Fiction writing workshop. The only rule was the story had to feature a cupid. Being me, I wanted to do something other than the cute cherub with his arrows of love. I also wanted to write something that might have been at home in one of the magazines of pulp's Golden Age. This delightful story about not-so-delightful critters is the result.

My family hails from the Appalachian coalfields of far southwest Virginia, where many old superstitions, traditions, and mountain lore still linger. *To Catch a Thief* was inspired by stories told by my great-grandmother, a feisty old mountain woman from the High Lonesome who made most of her own nostrums and medicines from local plants and her own special brand of magic.

Malaya is another story of traditional magic,

this time from the other side of the world. While set in the Appalachian mountains, the magic is definitely not local. Remember that you should never mess with a tiny woman who has big confidence.

I rarely write flash fiction. *Swift's* is by far my shortest piece, and another what-if story. In this case, what if someone read Jonathan Swift's *A Modest Proposal* and decided it made sense?

Birth of the Makmorn is one of those stories we sometimes write to answer our own questions. How did a character start out? What is his history? Where did she come from? The hero in this case will appear in another volume in the near future. This story stands alone, but some of you will remember Bran and his oath when the time comes.

Enough rambling from me. Dig in, O Reader, and journey from the far future back into the hoary mists of the Long Ago. Along the way, make sure to pick up some snacks for the road.

For more stories, check out www.JasonAdams Books.com, where you can sign up for my newsletter and keep up with the squirrel shenanigans.

In closing, let me say that I truly appreciate your interest and support. No story is complete until it is read by you, O Reader.

Thank you for completing mine.

TALES FROM THE SQUIRREL GARDEN

ANGEL OF MERCY

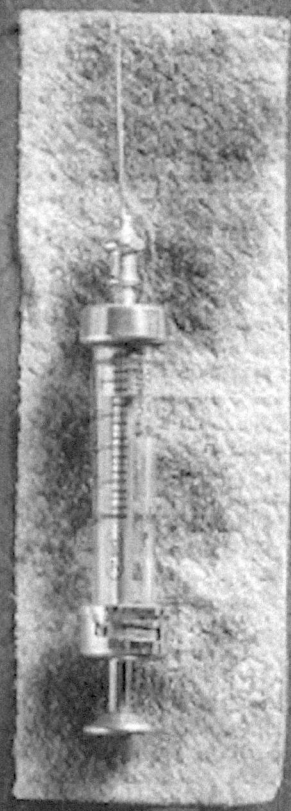

JASON A. ADAMS
Author of *Agonist* and *To Catch a Thief*

For Kari, who talked me into giving this writing thing a try.

CHAPTER 1

MARCH 23, 1917 – Arras, France

THE DANK WARD stank of urine, feces, sweat, ammonia, infection—the assorted reeks of a body that didn't know it should be dead.

Gray tunnels carved from the living granite stretched away to the edges of the incredible underground city which protected the Allied soldiers in this hospital where so many of them wept and died. The corridors and rooms had once been electrified, but were lit now by the smoky yellow flames of kerosene lanterns, dancing from time to time with the tremors caused by the massive barrages along the Western Front, felt deep in the bones even from ten miles away. The electric had proved too unreliable, so wires and Edison bulbs had been removed somewhere else. Where, the dead neither knew nor cared.

A woman sat beside one of the stained cots, holding the occupant's clammy, unresponsive hand, the only part of the poor soldier not broken and bloody. She stroked it, softly crooning a lullaby only half-remembered, one her father used to sing to her.

He was always with her at times like this, when she gave the gift no one but her had had the courage or holiness to give her Pa after a rockfall broke his back and his head, leaving him a drooling idiot confined to his bed until she sent him to walk with the Lord.

Her chosen this evening looked to be about nineteen years old. What remained of his hair was fine yellow cornsilk strands, matted here and there by his crimson blood. She imagined that he had been a strong, handsome young man. His determined eyes and brave heart now dimmed by the whims of fate and shrapnel.

It was time.

She leaned down and placed a soft kiss on the forehead of the young man. She sat back and tasted him on her lips, a little salty from the sweat beading all over his body, the body which betrayed his everlasting soul and happiness by refusing to die.

She thought of all the kisses he would never know, the kisses young women would never know from him, all of them stolen by a German artillery shell.

With his dog tags missing and half his face gone, the woman didn't know who he was. Someone's son, surely. Possibly a husband or lover. Perhaps a Pa that some poor child would remember only as a blurred image, lost to time and the savagery of war.

Or a hero. She liked that. He would be a hero for her, if for no one else.

She looked around, making sure she was alone save for those who could never betray her presence, then slipped the needle of a polished brass syringe under stitches which were not able to stop the blood leaking from the shattered bones where his lower jaw once hung.

Morphine had given him respite from pain. Now she gave him respite from life as a maimed and disfigured cripple. She was his angel, as she had been for all the others. Surely they would stand at God's side and thank her when she met them again in Heaven.

She took his hand again, caressing the palm and fingers, humming her Pa's beautiful song until the soldier's chest heaved upward, then settled back. His labored breathing finally stopped. She could feel his blessing in her heart as his soul was released from its prison.

CHAPTER 2

October 4, 1919 – New Orleans

Ted Mooney, newly appointed Captain of the New Orleans Police Department's 1st District, was having second thoughts about accepting his promotion.

He'd been called down to the derelict Storyville area, supposedly cleaned up by Mayor Behrman back in '17, but still running its various vice dens undercover. More dead bodies had been found, and the mayor was after him to find the cause.

Ted walked along the filthy, rubbish-strewn alley behind Conti Street, kicking up clouds of noxious foulness as he waded through the piles of rotting garbage and over rotting drunks and opium eaters. His watch read two-thirty, but time didn't matter down here. Bottles and pockets emptied all day and all night under the glowing red lights.

Sergeant LeCroix, the local beat officer, stood beside a tarp, the humped shapes underneath unmistakably human.

"What do we have, Lee?" Ted said, lifting an edge of the stained cloth. "More fever victims?"

"I don' think so, me," LeCroix said. "These got no sign of the sickness."

Under the tarp lay two pitiful corpses. Young girls, maybe sixteen or seventeen, wearing only tattered bawdy-house dresses and torn hose.

"Do we know who they were?"

"They worked the creole cribs for Miz White," LeCroix said. "The older one is called Daphne, the other was Sadie. No idea if those are real names or not. You want me to bring Miz White in again?"

"No point. She's got the judge well paid for."

Ted looked around, scratching his chin and trying to block the smell of decay from his mind. Poor kids. Life wasn't as hard for the colored in New Orleans as in other parts of the South, but it was still difficult. So many had no skills to offer an employer but what they could do on their backs.

He took a deep breath, held it, then knelt to examine the bodies. He hoped he wouldn't lose the lunch he could taste in the back of his throat. He felt shame at his own embarrassment.

He was still alive.

No signs of violence, besides bite marks from the rats and other hungry inhabitants of the back alleys. Nothing in their faces of fright or surprise. Or of peace. He'd heard people talk of the dead as looking asleep, but he always thought they just looked dead.

"How many is that since June, Lee? Twenty-six?"

"Something like, Boss."

"This ain't sickness, and it's not stabbing or shooting. No broken bones or strangulation, either. For all that, I'd bet my left arm this isn't natural."

He stood again, dropping the cloth back into place. "Take them to the mortuary, Lee. I'm going to ask around."

CHAPTER 3

TED WALKED SLOWLY to Lulu White's Saloon, thinking along the way. There was no damn rhyme or reason here.

No policeman in the Big Easy was shocked by corpses in the streets and alleyways. Rivers of bootleg liquor floated rafts of every other vice under the sun. That didn't make for quiet nights on the veranda for a huge chunk of the inhabitants, especially near the river.

But these dead folks were different. A lot of them were prostitutes, to be sure, but there were also men and children. They didn't seem to have anything in common, except all were from poorer circumstances. Some had missing limbs. Others had the rotting flesh of syphilitic dissipation. Still others were just destitute people living as best they could on the street. No one anyone would miss, but still...

At the corner of Conti and Basin, he bumped into Sister Rose as she was leaving one of the ratty tenements.

"Afternoon, Sister," he said, steadying her by the shoulders. "How's the day finding you?"

"Oh, hello Inspector—I mean *Captain* Mooney," she said, beaming up at him with her lovely eyes, the color of sun-kissed emerald. "I was so pleased to hear you were given such a wonderful advance. God surely smiles upon you."

The tiny nun probably weighed ninety pounds soaking wet. Her head barely reached his neck, and she was thin as a broomstraw. But she had grit and the strength to minister to the needs of the city's destitute in a way which had earned her the respect of high and low alike. As far as he knew, she belonged to no particular Order or Church. She was an independent and seemed glad to stay such.

"Thank you kindly, ma'am. I'm pleased to have the trust."

She walked beside him for a while, chatting idly about the weather, occasionally tucking stray bits of red hair back under her wimple. Ted snuck a glance or two out the corner of his eye, not able to help thinking what a fine woman she'd make him if she'd ever take off that damn church garb. She was around his age, judging by what he could see of her face, and the lightweight fabric of her hot-weather habit clung here and there as she walked in a way that—

He coughed, and turned his eyes forward again. "I'm sorry, Sister, what did you say?" He hoped he wasn't blushing. He was a product of Catholic School upbringing, and shouldn't be thinking of the Sister that way.

"I asked if you were making any headway on the unfortunate murders the District has seen these last few months."

They waited on the corner while a maroon streetcar rattled by, then he took her elbow as they crossed the avenue. He was surprised at the strength he felt in her slender arm.

"We're sure working on it," he said. "Not much to go on, really. Have you heard or seen anything? People might talk to you easier than to one of us."

"I have not, but I'll listen for you," she said, stopping halfway down the block. "I must leave you here, I'm afraid. There's a sick mother inside." She looked at the battered door of a cheap apartment house, the paint a sun-baked no-color peeling from the walls. Half the windows were bare of glass, and twinkling shards littered the gutter below. "This is not one of my favorite stops, but the poor dear has young children. I hope we can pull her through, with our Savior's aid."

"You're truly an angel, Sister Rose," he said. "It amazes me what all you're able to do for folks."

"It's my calling, Captain," she said, giving him a peculiar smile. "I've known what I was meant for since caring for my father during his final months."

"Well, I'll surely be sending good thoughts your way," he said, watching her up the stairs and inside.

CHAPTER 4

LULU WHITE'S Saloon was in full swing when Ted arrived. Patrons of every race and class thronged the smoke-filled interior as a raucous jazz band blatted and thumped on the stage. He could barely hear himself think.

He wove through the milling crowd, jostled by whites and coloreds alike, wearing everything from rough dockworker's dungarees stinking of rotting fish to fancy silk waistcoats, silver watch chains sewn to the pockets to thwart greedy fingers. The bright buzz of sparklights cut through the general noise, and Ted wondered how Lulu had been able to swing electrifying this place after Mahogany Hall, her main brothel, was shut down.

Lulu was holding court in a curved corner settee, her brown face striking above an ivory gown. Long white gloves covered her arms, her wrists and fingers bedecked with diamonds, emeralds, and rubies. Her jewelry was far too gaudy to be fake.

He stepped to the table, ignoring the contemptuous looks from the swells who surrounded the famous Madam. "Miz White? Mind if I ask you a few questions?"

"Why, Captain Theodore Mooney," she said, her voice genteel and friendly, her smile not reaching her eyes. "Whatever brings you to my establishment? Are you boys getting thirsty out there in all this unseasonable heat? Shall I have one of the girls bring you some cool refreshment?"

"Not at all, ma'am," he said, "although I do thank you for the offer."

"Please, take a seat," She turned to one of the rich boys. "William, be a dear and give the officer some room."

"That won't be necessary. I'm only here to tell you we found a couple of your girls dead. Daphne and Sadie."

Lulu closed her eyes for a moment, then looked straight at him. "How did they die, Ted?"

"We don't know for sure, Lulu. I was hoping you might have some ideas. Were they sick?"

"In a way," she said. "Both came to me to let me know they'd gotten more than money from their work."

"So they both caught pregnant?"

"They both had growths, and they asked for

help getting them removed," she said delicately. Abortion was a regular occurrence among her employees, but it was still illegal and *not* to be discussed. "I gave them the name of someone who could help. That was day before yesterday."

Things kept getting worse. Two dead babes to add to the two dead children who carried them.

"Miz White—Lulu—will you tell me who you sent them to?"

"My helper in such matters is no murderer, Captain." Lulu had wrapped her dignity back around herself. "She is a pagan hoodoo woman, but not one to violate others."

"That may be," he said. "But if she can give me any information that helps us stop this from happening again, I need to talk to her." He took her gloved right hand in his. "Please, Lulu. We've known each other a long time, and you know I can't abide more dead youngsters."

Lulu searched his face, eyes narrowed. Finally she said, "Don't worry none about the hoodoo lady. They never got there. They wanted to go for absolution first."

"You think a priest is involved?"

"I don't know about any priest," she said. "I sent them to Sister Rose. I thought they'd be more comfortable with another woman, even if the Sister can't officially hear confession."

"Sister Rose? She—"

He stopped, thinking back to his conversation with the diminutive nun earlier. She'd asked him about the murders.

Did anyone outside the police community know the deaths might be murders?

CHAPTER 5

TED RAN BACK the way he'd come, blowing his whistle for all he was worth. LeCroix was the first he saw, still on the beat after his unpleasant chore.

"Lee!" he shouted. "Round up a couple more boys and meet me on Basin, between Conti and Bienville! The rundown building on the west side with all the broken windows!"

He ran on, arriving out of breath, dripping with sweat, and already hearing wailing from the third floor.

Ted held the ribs on his left side where a stitch was trying to double him over. He entered the ramshackle building, taking the stairs two at a time, zeroing in on the screams.

On the third floor, at the end of a dim hallway crisscrossed with narrow dust-filled shafts of light, a door stood open. A tall black woman wearing charwoman's garb stood just inside, hands at her throat as she shrieked out the names of Saint after Saint.

Ted did not want to go in there. He didn't want confirmation.

He heard footsteps over the screams, and turned to see LeCroix coming up the stairs, followed by two burly boyos he knew by face but not by name yet. All three looked at him, eyebrows raised.

Ted drew a deep breath and let it out.

"Come on. No sense putting it off any longer."

One of the boys, Abercrombie according to his badge, gently pulled the screaming woman back and guided her down the hall, trying to shush her as they went. Ted, LeCroix, and the one whose badge said Deveraux walked in.

A smell of urine and feces hung in the air, the odors of recent death.

The apartment was only one room, with a coal stove and a few battered cabinets along one wall, a couple of cots along another, and a larger bed in the far corner.

The bed was a lovely item, with a tall black oaken headboard and footboard, the posts hand-carved, by some long-ago relative most likely, and a deep mattress sack. A beautiful crazy quilt dressed the bed in a riot of joyful color.

On top of the quilt lay a skinny creole woman in her shift, the marks of disease on her greying face.

Her arms were crossed on her breast, her hand holding a small wooden crucifix.

On either side of her, tucked against her still frame as though for warmth, lay two little boy-children. Their pale cheeks were drawn with hunger, but they would never again feel those pangs.

Ted started to speak, but had to clear his throat a couple of times. He didn't bother wiping the tears away as they coursed down his cheeks. Beside him, the two other policemen crossed themselves and muttered prayers in French patois.

"Lee," he finally said. "I was too late. I don't want to be too late again."

"What you want us to do, Boss?" LeCroix said. He looked straight at Ted, avoiding the tableau before them.

"I need you to get everyone out on the street. Go church to church, up every alley, into every building. Find a small white nun named Sister Rose. Find me once you do."

"Sè Rosie?" LeCroix said. "Don't say it, Captain! She's a saint to these people!"

"I don't think so, Lee. For right now, I just want to talk to her. Go on, now."

Deveraux stayed behind to wait for the meat wagon, while Ted and LeCroix went downstairs, then headed in different directions.

CHAPTER 6

THE OCTOBER SUN was already on the way down and the lamplighter was making his way along Basin Street. Ted walked north along the avenue, not hurrying his steps, hoping one of the other men would find the Sister.

So far, he had nothing to go on but a feeling in his gut. A sick feeling, to be sure. Suspecting a woman of the cloth was a wee bit different than going after a roughneck in the back of a saloon. Still, though...

In cases like these, gut feelings were usually worth more than a wheelbarrow load of harder evidence.

Ted finally arrived at a small, clean building. *Bates Hardware* curved above the door, the paint a well-kept and jaunty red. Just past a display window full of various garden and carpentry tools, a narrow and well-built stair rose to the upper story, where an oil lamp shone from a spotless window hung with plain white curtains.

He tried to lay aside his childish fear of accosting the clergy and pull the authority of Captain Mooney around himself as he climbed the stairs. All he wanted to do was ask some questions, right? There was most likely nothing the tiny nun could tell him.

Right?

He knocked, and the door opened right away. She must have heard him on the stairs.

"Why, hello Captain," she said, beaming again. "What a pleasant surprise. Do come in. Would you like a cool glass of tea? I was just about to make some dinner, I hope you can stay."

She stepped back and he entered cautiously, still feeling like a schoolboy in the Mother Superior's office.

He looked around the small and tidy kitchen, and noticed a row of shelves covered with dark brown carboys and bottles. Several of them had medical labels, and one that looked to hold about a quart was nearly half empty.

The label filled his sight.

Morphine.

"Now then, what can I do for you?" she said, handing him a tall glass.

He started to take a drink, then thought better of

it and just held the glass. He looked down at Sister Rose, at those gorgeous green eyes, and licked his lips.

"Sister, I don't know how to put this. There were some deaths in that building I left you at earlier. A mother and two small children."

"Yes, poor dears," she said bustling around the kitchen, putting pots on the stove and pulling boxes and tins from the cabinets. "Her consumption kept getting worse and she was in dreadful pain, but she's with the Almighty now, she and her boys."

Ted gaped at her. "Did you...I mean, what happened?"

"I could see she would never get better. I asked her if she accepted our Savior as her own, and she did. We prayed for a while, and I could see her soul was clean, so I helped her escape the prison of disease and travel to her reward."

She smiled a beatific smile, cool and serene as one of the old statues in St. Louis Cathedral.

"My God," Ted said. "And those poor children?"

"Tsk, Captain. Surely you can see they are better off with our Lord than they would be starving on the streets or in some orphanage?"

His hand trembled violently as he set the glass down, slopping brown liquid onto the neat tablecloth. Sister Rose showed no remorse, no regret.

Just the calm peace of one who truly believes in their own righteousness.

His right hand dropped to the worn rubber grip of his service revolver as he felt competing instincts urging him to stop this madness, or to shoot the monster standing before him.

"Did you kill all the others too?" he said, his voice shaking.

"No, of course not," she said, turning back to the cabinets, rummaging in the drawers. "Some of them died of drink, drugs, or disease. I only help the ones who are ready to enter Heaven with a clean conscience."

He drew his pistol and pointed it at the black cloth covering her small back.

"Sister Rose, I am placing you under arrest for the three murders this afternoon, and as many others as you may have committed. Raise your hands and move away from the stove."

She turned to face him, her face growing stern when she saw the gun.

"Theodore!" she snapped. "Stop your foolishness and put that away!"

A hand trained by years of Catholic School started to drop, but he rallied and held fast.

"Please, Sister. Don't make this harder than need be."

She moved toward him, wagging the index finger of her left hand in his face like she'd just caught him putting some girl's pigtails in the inkwell.

Her right hand was hidden in the folds of her habit.

"Do you think I will stop doing God's work simply because you say so?" she said, her voice growing heated. "I *saved* those people from the world's evil! I let them get to Heaven with sin-free souls! You should *thank* me for making your job easier!"

He backed away in the face of her displeasure, the pistol still held between them.

He bumped into the wall, but she kept coming.

"You have no authority over me and my work!" Spittle sprayed from her lips. Her green eyes were no longer lovely. Now they blazed with holy fervor. "God's children will not be denied release from the sins of this Earth just because—"

Her right hand suddenly shot forward, whipping a gleaming glass syringe toward his neck.

He jerked back, finger tightening spasmodically on the trigger, firing three shots in rapid succession.

The bullets punched through her frail body like an icepick through newsprint, shattering the windows behind her and spraying the wall with blood.

She stared at him, then looked down at the smoking holes in the ebony cloth.

"Oh my God," Mooney said, catching her as she

started to fall. He had enough presence of mind to pluck the syringe from her relaxing fingers as he laid her carefully on the floor.

Blood ran from her mouth, the pink froth telling of ruined lungs.

He heard the holes in her chest whistling, and knew there was nothing anyone could do for her.

"Sister Rose, I wish you hadn't made me do that,"

He didn't know how to feel. He'd acted in self-defense, but that didn't make shooting a nun any easier.

He was amazed to see her smiling.

"I forgive you," she whispered. Frothy blood bubbled from her lips as she spoke. "I will be beside the Lord Jesus soon, with all those who went before me there to welcome me Home."

Mooney couldn't find anything to say as her breath slowed, then stopped. Blood pooled out from underneath her body, running in crimson rills toward the wall. In the distance, he could hear the shrill whistles of his fellow officers, summoning assistance that would arrive far too late to help anyone.

CHAPTER 7

TED, still a Captain by some miracle, left Superintendent Boyle's office two days later. LeCroix was waiting for him, and they left City Hall together.

Both men wore their parade dress, buttons and leather polished and gleaming in the early October sun. The heat wave had finally broken, and Ted tried not to link *that* with the end of a certain killing spree.

"Well, Boss?" LeCroix said. "We going to celebrate, or to mourn?"

"Hell Lee, I don't know. Let's just get a drink and let everyone else decide what it means."

They shared an uneasy and self-conscious chuckle as they headed for Lulu White's place. After the details went public, Ted was a bit of a pariah among many of New Orleans' Catholic community, among those who refused to believe anything bad about Sister Rose.

But Lulu had told him he never needed to count his coins before coming to her place.

The two men stopped in front of the saloon and stood looking at all the passers-by. Rich, poor, young, old, white, colored—a snapshot of the world right under their noses.

"How you feeling, Ted?" LeCroix asked in his gentle Creole accent.

"I don't rightly know, Lee. Sister Rose was sure she was doing the right thing. I have no idea if shooting her was the right thing or not, and I guess I never will until I'm standing at the Throne and it's too late."

"I been a cop a long time, me," LeCroix said. "I tell you this, Ted. If ever I know for sure what the right thing is, no question, I hope you do me the favor of shooting me as well."

He clapped LeCroix on the shoulder as they walked through Lulu's doors.

Ted was more than happy to leave the world outside for a while.

The
GREEN KNIGHT

JASON A. ADAMS

To Cú Chulainn, Gawain, and all the other suckers.

CHAPTER 1

GAVIN COULDN'T STOP TREMBLING.

He walked quickly down the noisy Buckhead street, eyes darting over every face, looking for the accusation he knew he would eventually find. He could smell his own fear-sweat as the muggy Atlanta night tried to suffocate him in a wet blanket of heat, still eighty degrees even at one in the morning.

On the road, cars went past with few gaps. Atlanta traffic didn't stop when the sun went down. On the sidewalks, drunk kids went by in both directions, looking for the next bar or the next hooker. A normal, everyday night in this pocket of bars and bistros.

How had he gotten mixed up in this mess? Gavin Baddock, Attorney at Law. Shyster at work, more like. He had no illusions about himself. He was simply a lawsuit chaser, helping con artists milk the system any way they could.

When Carl Grunnecht came to him with a misuse of persona claim against some beer company called Green Knight Brewery, Gavin hadn't cared one bit about the particulars, just how he could make the silly claim work.

Carl was a huge brute of a man, easily 6'5 and broad as a barn. His shaggy mane and beard curled redly over shoulders and chest, and he had an odd accent that Gavin couldn't place. Not quite Irish, not quite German.

But it was the story the big man spun that convinced Gavin he was crazy.

Carl had rattled on and on about fairies and party tricks, a fortune made during the French Revolution, working with magicians in Vegas, all utter raving as far as Gavin could tell.

It wasn't until Carl invited him to his home that his world had collapsed.

Gavin had walked into a museum of beheading. Axes, swords, and a huge guillotine decorated Carl's shabby apartment, which stank of a strange coppery reek that made Gavin's gorge rise.

When the giant lay down with his head in the guillotine and handed him the rope, Gavin played along, trying to humor him. But when he yanked the release, the huge, gleaming blade fell with a horribly final "thunk" and Carl's head dropped into the waiting basket.

Gavin had frozen with shock for what felt like hours but in truth was only a minute or so.

Then he'd run. Down the stairs, out to the sidewalk, down toward the lights and hubbub of the real world.

Gavin finally felt safe enough to stop and catch his breath. As he opened the door to a ubiquitous Waffle House, meaning to grab some coffee to clear his head, a huge meaty paw fell on his shoulder.

"Vy you run avay, Mr. Baddock?"

Gavin looked up at the shaggy head, ran through several possible responses, and finally did the only sensible thing.

He passed out.

CHAPTER 2

AN HOUR LATER, Gavin sat at Carl's dinner table, wondering if he or his giant host were the crazier.

"So you're telling me you're the *actual* Green Knight? Like in the King Arthur stories?"

"Of course. You t'ink all dem stories just make beleef? Two t'ousand years, and you t'ink I get so much as von penny from dose damn storytellers? It is such shit, I tell you true!"

Gavin stared in fascination, seeing the faint red line around Carl's neck. He looked over at the guillotine, at the dark stain below the wooden notch. The guy might turn out to be a con artist, but it was sure one hell of a trick.

"So...what is it you want me to do? I'm not sure we can prove you're the *real* Green Knight..." Wheels were grinding back to life in Gavin's mind, reminding him that he also was just a con artist of sorts.

"Look. I don't know if we can get anything from a beer company. I mean, it's not like you have a registered trademark on Green Knight." He stood and began to pace. "We might be able to score pretty big, though...wrongful death...reckless endangerment..."

"Vat you talk about, Mr. Baddock? I'm not dead. I cannot die. I t'ought I showed you such."

"Yeah, but..." Gavin stopped his muttering and pacing. He was seeing himself in a Maserati, trophy girl du jour beside him. Nice big house on West Paces Ferry. Penthouse office in Midtown.

"Listen to me, Carl. No one besides me knows about your...um...*talent*, right?"

"Vell, Oberon does. Votan, T'or, few odders."

Gavin blinked, then put the names out of his mind. One demigod was enough for now.

"I don't think we have to worry about them spilling your beans." He sat back at the table, leaning forward slightly with hands clasped, his I'm-a-real-lawyer-you-can-trust-me pose.

"We can get *rich*, Carl. I mean filthy, stinking, obscenely rich! We get you a wife who can play the poor widow. We arrange your accidental beheading every few months. Sue some poor slob...no, no individuals. Some poor *corporation* for your death and your bereft widow's pain and suffering."

Gavin didn't see the apartment with its weird décor anymore. He was seeing an end to chasing ambulances and car wrecks. An end to wondering how he'd ever pay off his house and student loan. An end to everything except a wonderful life of luxury.

"Ah, I see," Carl said, smiling broadly. "So you dream of vealth and glory?"

"Who doesn't?" Gavin looked at Carl, wondering if the big guy was serious. "Who doesn't want to rise above? The desire for excellence, the drive to succeed, the hope that we can make ourselves better. That's what makes us human."

"Dat has forever been true," Carl agreed. "Hokay. Ve can vork togedder. But, you vill need to always be dere to collect me, if I am playing dead. I don't vant to spend no more time in cold freezer boxes dan I haf to."

"We'll need to find a couple of paramedics we can trust—"

"No! YOU be the ambulance driver. Find cops who don't ask kvestions if dey are paid. You can do de correct papers ve vill need?"

Finally! Something he was confident about. "Oh, sure. No problem. I've been doing my own medical records for cases for years. I know a couple of people in all the courthouses."

City officials in the Metro Atlanta area did not get paid well at all.

Not by the city, anyway.

"Good!" Carl said. "Vy don't ve start here? Dis bastard landlord has alvays been an asshole. I vill enjoy taking his money for nothing, instead of de odder vay around for a change."

CHAPTER 3

TEN DAYS LATER, Gavin waited around the corner in a grungy old ambulance he'd gotten at a hospital auction, and an EMT uniform he'd cadged from a client who still owed him a couple of thousand bucks. He wasn't sure what Carl had in mind, he was just supposed to wait until he heard screaming from the little receiver velcroed to the dashboard.

Carl had the microphone, disguised as a wrist-watch. Amazing what you could get on the Internet these days.

Gavin jumped when the receiver squawked.

"Be ready, Mr. Baddock. Vait two minutes after de racket begins so dey haf time to call de nine-von-vons."

Then Gavin grabbed the receiver and spun the volume down as the cab of the meatwagon filled with shrieks and screams. Whatever he'd done, Carl must have waited until there was a good-sized crowd around.

Gavin gave it three minutes, then snatched up a realistic-looking equipment box and ran into the apartment building. Some people were hysterical, some were quietly weeping. Most had their cell phones out taking pictures and video.

Carl's big body lay in front of the elevator, neck right up against the doors. Gavin ran over, knelt down, and grabbed Carl's wrist, hoping he looked like he was taking a pulse. Not that there was any need to.

"Dude, don't bother," a scruffy looking twenty something in a Famous Ron's Pizza uniform said. "This guy don't have a head anymore."

"What happened?" Gavin asked, pulling a notebook from his box.

"The elevator opened early, man," the kid replied. "Big dude here stuck his head in, looking for the elevator I guess, and it came down and clipped him." He gave a shaky laugh. "Closest haircut he ever got."

Gavin stood and looked the crowd over. "Where's the head?" He took the kid's shoulder. "Go down to the ambulance and bring up the gurney from the back."

He flapped his hands at the crowd, shooing them back, then found the stairs and pelted down to the basement level. He found the correct elevator and was just able to prize the doors halfway open. There in the bottom of the shaft, between the safety springs, lay Carl's head, facing upward.

The eyes rolled toward him, and the left eye dropped him a wink.

Gavin picked the gruesome object up with both hands and carried it back up to the lobby. The pizza guy was back with the gurney. The kid, as well as the gaggle of onlookers gaped at Gavin's burden. Some went pale and turned aside, hands to mouths. Others kept their phones trained on him.

The kid just pointed and said, "Dude! That's fuckin' gnarly!" He'd be up for his Pulitzer in no time, Gavin thought, trying not to laugh.

He collapsed the gurney, thankful he'd taken the time to practice with it. Between himself, the pizza guy, and a couple of the less squeamish men in the crowd, they hoisted Carl's body onto the stretcher. Gavin placed the head gently against the bloody stump of Carl's neck, then pulled the sheet over the whole mess.

As he rolled the gurney away, he called out to the crowd.

"Some of you need to stay here for when the police arrive. Tell them I've taken the body to the morgue at Grady Hospital."

Then he was out the door, over to the rear of the ambulance, loading the gurney, and finally in the driver's seat with the door closed and locked.

He turned on the rolling lights, but not the siren, and drove south toward the hospital. After a couple of blocks, Gavin switched the lights back off, and turned at the next corner, driving back to his office. He nearly swerved off the road when Carl stepped forward and sank into the passenger seat.

"Dat vas fun," said the clearly not deceased giant. "Is alvays a laff to shock de rubes."

"I saw your body and your head, loaded you up, and still I'm having a hard time believing it. You'll have to tell me the secret someday."

"Tell you vat. Ve met on August 6, yes? You come ask me again same day next year."

Gavin laughed and replied, "It's a date! In the meantime, let's see what we can do about a landlord who obviously was endangering the safety of his tenants. Plus, we have to make arrangements for your stuff." Carl had written out a will leaving everything he owned to Gavin, who would return it all, of course.

CHAPTER 4

THEY GOT close to a million bucks from the building's owners, forty percent of which went to Gavin. Well, all of it went to him as Carl's beneficiary, but he only kept the forty. He wasn't unethical and wouldn't take more than his usual contingency percentage.

Over the next twelve months, they used Carl's remarkable abilities to collect from building owners, trucking companies (Carl lost his head when a semi turned in front of his motorcycle and the trailer got him), helicopter pilots—any and all who could conceivably decapitate someone by arranged and careful accident.

By the time August rolled back around, Gavin had collected close to twenty-three million dollars, each time taking his forty percent cut.

There had been some close calls, some suspicions that he and Carl were working a scam, but they'd been very careful. They'd only pulled the first one in the Atlanta area. The others had been done in Chattanooga, Birmingham, Savannah, and Miami. Good size cities, with little chance of anyone being able to positively ID either Gavin or Carl.

Plus, there was the undeniable fact that Carl had his head on his shoulders, and was walking, breathing, and certainly wasn't dead. Hard to make a case on a guy who refused to stay a corpse.

CHAPTER 5

ON AUGUST SEVENTH, exactly one year after meeting Carl Grunnecht for the first time, Gavin parked his Maserati outside Carl's current abode. He didn't have a trophy girl with him this evening, but there had been plenty of willing companions over the last twelve months, yes indeed. Tonight was a stag night, however, partners only. They were going out on the town tonight to celebrate their success with good food, good booze, friendly strippers, the whole nine yards.

He rang the bell, and Carl opened up and invited him in. Carl wore a suit that had to contain a clipper ship's worth of cloth, but which fit his massive frame well. Gavin saw a couple of highball glasses on the table, already holding three fingers of what smelled like some excellent bourbon.

Carl handed him one, took the other, and said,

"Let us toast our success, my good friend." They tapped their glassed together with a musical *clink* of fine crystal.

"And to many more years of successful litigation," Gavin replied, then drained his glass. Yes, an excellent bourbon. Good vanilla flavor, nice and oaken body, some sort of bitter undertones.

"Another glass, then off to the depraved fleshpots of this modern Sodo…"

Funny. Everything was spinning.

He couldn't…

"Carl?"

Gavin dropped his glass on the way down to the floor.

CHAPTER 6

GAVIN ROSE BACK UP to consciousness. He came to fairly quickly, and was able to open his eyes only moments after awareness returned.

He still couldn't move, though.

"Ah, my good Mr. Baddock." Carl's voice, no mistaking it. "You are avake again? Good!"

Gavin was on his stomach, on some hard surface, and could barely raise his head to Carl's knees. What was going on?

"What happened? I think I passed out."

Carl knelt down until Gavin could see his face. "No, no. You did not pass out, Mr. Baddock. I drugged you to sleep. Dat is alvays easier when de time comes."

"What? You *drugged* me? What the hell?"

Gavin tried to get up, but his wrists were tied.

So were his ankles. And his chest. He was strapped down to a large board of some kind.

"Untie me, dammit! I'll—"

"Shhhh, Mr. Baddock. I like you and haf enjoyed our partnership, but dis must be done."

Carl stood and scooted a full length oval mirror in front of the helpless lawyer, tilting it so Gavin could see that he was bound to the same guillotine he'd seen Carl in on that long-ago night.

"It is after midnight," Carl said. "Vich means von year and a day since you cut my head off. Today is my turn."

Gavin saw him take the pull rope in hand.

"Wait!" Gavin said, horrorstruck. "We're partners! Besides, I came to you of my own free will, so you're supposed to let me live!"

"Mr. Baddock, von reason I do not like de damn storytellers is dey alvays got at least von t'ing wrong."

Gavin felt Carl's big hand take his now sweaty one and shake.

"T'ank you for a fun year and a day, but dis is vat I haff to do to keep de magic vorking."

"Goodbye, Mr. Baddock."

Carl pulled the rope.

There was a swish, a thunk, and a room full of antique murder devices tumbling upward.

There was one final thought.

He conned me.

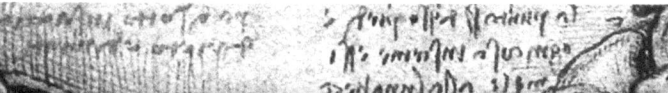

OPPOSITIONAL

JASON A. ADAMS

To all the fans of medical studies.

CHAPTER 1

PHILLIP DEGRANZ DIDN'T TRUST the house.

He stood in the center of the long drive, the scents of foxglove, nicotiana, thistle, and many more herbs and flowers combined with the underlying odor of the septic's leach field. The flower beds had once been well-maintained, but obviously not for a long while.

Phillip felt as though he were staring up a primordial tunnel, the extravagant growth arching above and closing in from the sides. The manor itself could be seen standing at the end of the tunnel, silently insulting the world with its aura of slowly moldering grandeur.

At first, Phillip couldn't understand his strong reaction. Perhaps it was the way the bright sunlight seemed to shrink away from the windows, afraid to pass through the glass and into whatever rooms lay beyond.

But no, he believed it was the way there were too many shadows, more than the various angles and outcroppings of the ancient stone pile could account for. Or perhaps it was just the lingering taste of bitter, overbrewed tea and burnt sausages that had him feeling off kilter.

Poor Margaret. She was a lovely girl and he felt lucky to have won her, but after only several weeks of marriage she was still learning the domestic arts necessary for a happy and well-run home.

Phillip remembered his meeting with Dougal MacOwen earlier that week. He had heard MacOwen's name at various university functions, but knew little more than that he was financially very kind to the school, and had some unusual theories regarding skeletal manipulation and its role in the healing of various disorders.

Phillip had been surprised and flattered when his secretary passed along MacOwen's request for an interview. The man had been the soul of gentility, asking after Phillip and his family, discussing upcoming conferences and lectures, as well as expounding on his various interests, including anatomy.

"There are between 206 and 270 bones in the human body, dependent upon age and gender," he'd said. "With the proper application of oppositional torque, any one of them may be broken without disturbing its neighbors. Several excellent minds are developing the technique to assist in the resetting of improperly healed fractures. A noble cause, wouldn't you say?"

The man's smile hadn't changed a whit during this speech.

MacOwen had then gone on to explain his daughter's troubles with osteitis, and how he had been drawn into curiosity and then partnership with her physicians before and after her unfortunate death from the disease. He had gone into some detail of her deformities, asking if Phillip had ever seen examples of such, although he had to admit his inexperience to the older man.

Phillip had been quite impressed with MacOwen's command of the subject, and when invited to come see his home and laboratory, had readily accepted.

After time to consider MacOwen's interests, and his strangely cool charm, Phillip had begun to wonder if his acceptance had been too hasty.

Perhaps he should have stayed at home this morning.

CHAPTER 2

HE KNEW he wasn't himself at breakfast. Margaret was worrying over him like a mother hen.

The shy and awkward daughter of his old physiology professor had blossomed into a delightfully winsome young lady, but also one who had no truck with introverted academics.

"What troubles you about this meeting?" she finally asked.

"I don't know, my pet," Phillip replied. "Something about the man...his eyes, I suppose. MacOwen is certainly knowledgeable about osteology, and says he wishes to make a large grant in return for being allowed access to our facilities, but..."

"Osteology?" Now her brow furrowed in the charmingly childlike way which made her seem so much younger than her nineteen years. "I think I've heard you mention the word. The study of bones, isn't it?"

Phillip pulled his young wife onto his lap and tickled along her ribs. "*Human* bones, Angel. The study of lovely skeletons like yours." Phillip hands tickled her more strategically as he tried to turn teasing into something more, but she squealed and leapt up.

"You, sir, are a cad. You may be the youngest Proctor at the University, but you should have been Professor of Knavery!" She drew him to his feet, gave him a hug and warm kiss, then set his hat on his head. "Now go meet with this generous benefactor, my love, and come home a more learned and successful husband."

A final kiss and embrace, and Phillip waved farewell from the hansom cab's window, already looking forward to his lovely bride's company that evening.

CHAPTER 3

AND SO PHILLIP WAS HERE. At this point it would be impolite, not to mention cowardly, not to ring the bell. Perhaps MacOwen had forgotten the appointment.

He walked toward the towering entry door, telling himself his lack of speed was due to his appreciation of the fine gardens.

He did not need to ring, however, as MacOwen opened the great black barrier, strapped and studded with heavy iron, just as Phillip gained the top of the stair.

"My dear DeGranz," he called, that same hatefully genial smile still avoiding his dark blue eyes. "Do come in and enjoy my home. I have been eagerly awaiting the chance to share my endeavors with you."

Phillip entered, studying every detail of the foyer in an attempt to reassure himself.

The attempt failed.

The thick rugs and heavy tapestries silenced their footfalls and deadened their voices. The room seemed quite dark in spite of the many windows surrounding the doorframe.

Three other doors led further into the belly of the house, all the same ironbound oak as that behind, which MacOwen now shut to with a reverberant boom like the final closing of the mausoleum.

His host opened the left-most door and stood like a manservant, his princely kilt and jacket at odds with his pose.

"My study," he said, motioning Phillip in. "I apologize for the absence of my man, but he left my service all of a sudden and I am still interviewing. Still though, I haven't forgot how to pour a proper whisky."

Phillip preceded the big Scot into a room filled with macabre failures of life. Glass jars covered every shelf and table, containing various alcohol-marinated monstrosities.

Here a poor babe with two legs, three arms, and a second head; there another infant with most of its skull and all of its brain missing; and on the desk a horrid example of cyclopia—a tiny body with only one eye, a slit of a mouth, and no other facial features at all.

He shuddered in disgust. He was a scientific man, but preferred case studies to these hideously immediate nightmares. Phillip had to focus on the fireplace to keep from tasting his breakfast anew.

"Marvelous, aren't they?" MacOwen asked as he busied himself with the whisky bottle. "The human form, supposedly made in the image of that god we cast in our own, and just look what Nature can do with Her blind randomness."

Phillip took his glass, and another quick glance at the gruesome collection. "Yes, I see. But MacOwen, however did you acquire such a collection?"

"Simplicity itself," replied his host as he sat in an overstuffed armchair by the cold fireplace and waved Phillip to its mate. "I have several friends in the medical community, as I am somewhat of a student of the *ars medica* myself. They sometimes gift me with interesting specimens in return for knowledge gleaned from my own humble osteological studies."

This was the moment when Phillip knew himself to be well and truly trapped.

In spite of his misgivings, he wouldn't be able to leave without seeing those experiments for himself, no matter how much he dreaded the revelation.

This obsessive curiosity had led him into grief more than once, but he could no more resist the compulsion than an eater of opium in some heathen den of vice.

"Where is your laboratory?" he heard himself ask, knowing he should instead run for the doors and freedom. "I would be honored to share in what you've discovered."

No help for it.

None at all.

MacOwen's smile finally changed, reaching his eyes at long last. "You are most kind. I was indeed hoping you would be willing to assist me in one or two small matters of osteology."

Here he rose and swung aside the seemingly solid fireplace to reveal a tiny portal, scarcely five feet high and two wide, heavily barred and shackled, which he unlocked with a cunningly intricate key.

They passed down the dark stone stairs, MacOwen's shoulders brushing either wall. The light from the lantern he held cast an ogre's shadow back over Phillip, who shivered with unease.

His trepidation was only increased by the dankness of the air and the steady drip-drip-drip of moisture from the low ceiling.

Finally, the stair ended at a broad landing before a huge bronze door, green with verdigris except for the highly polished lockplate and handle.

MacOwen swung the door open, the massive slab nearly silent on heavily greased hinges.

The two men stepped into a cavernous room, with cathedral arches of brickwork above, and black soapstone flags below. The chill darkness was vanquished by dozens of buzzing sparklights as MacOwen pulled a large, double-bladed switch on the wall.

The smell of the room nearly stopped Phillip in his tracks, like an aggressive and unprovoked blow to the face.

Astringent odors of vinegar and alcohol coated his nose and throat, along with an undercurrent of something organic yet foul, the smell of some wild beast's well-kept but long overused cage.

The odor then filled his mouth as he gasped in horror.

Nothing obviously gruesome was here, only the promise of gruesome acts to come.

Stocks and stays of various farrier's configurations were plainly meant to hold different animals in an array of poses, but it was the large medical examination table, gleaming copper set into a six-inch deep well over four drains, that most caught his eye.

The miasmic stench rising from these drains cut through the other aromas, invading his already outraged sensory cavities.

Then he noticed the chair.

It sat beside the table, a monstrous mockery of an invalid's wheelchair, with clamps for hand, feet, and head as well as straps for torso and thigh. The dark oak, ubiquitous in this place, was smooth and polished, but with an array of dark stains which Phillip prayed were only due to dampness and age.

His skin crawled its way into gooseflesh, every follicle drawing up in terror, and he felt the stabbing pain of a hypodermic needle between the fourth and fifth vertebrae at the nape of his neck.

The sensation lasted only the briefest of moments.

He lost his body only moments before his consciousness.

CHAPTER 4

HIS ENTIRE WORLD was agony now.

His bones had been broken one at a time over... hours? Days?

He had no idea.

Enough narcotic had been administered that he was denied the relief of pain-induced unconsciousness, but not so much that he didn't fully appreciate just how badly his body was being misused.

Phillip had to admit to himself that MacOwen's theory of oppositional torque was correct, as he felt and heard his left stirrup snap. The pain of the break wasn't really noticeable over that of the tiny pincer piercing his tympanic membrane.

Ah, Margaret. I would have enjoyed growing old with you.

"I hope the gallows man and then the Devil

show you the mercy you deserve, you inhuman bastard!"

"Don't be such a child," MacOwen said with a chuckle and an admonishing finger, cheerful as ever. "I am in as much danger from the Devil as I am from the Will O' the Wisp, and judges are quite inexpensive in my experience."

He was busy wiping down another specialty device, this one with a large turn-screw connected at ninety degrees to a blunt steel worm.

Phillip tried not to imagine which bone it was for.

"You will be a marvelous addition to science, and to my collection," MacOwen said, forcing his new horror into Phillip's mouth and turning the screw. "I shall be curious to see how your speech changes once your palatine bone splits."

Phillip thought about his lectures given at Oxford's anatomy department, soft words exchanged with his beautiful Margaret, the simple joy of singing a favorite tune.

With his jaws wrenched open he couldn't ask, but he rather hoped MacOwen would kill him soon.

As if reading his thoughts, MacOwen stopped twisting the device's screw.

"I have a wager on you, you know."

Twist.

"I bet 150 guineas that I can break 150 of your bones before the shock finally kills you."

Twist.

"Uunnnngh..." Phillip was confused, trying to plead for both mercy and an explanation, but could only manage animalistic grunts as the device simultaneously pressed against tongue and palate.

MacOwen leaned over him, staring directly into his eyes as he manipulated his hellish tool.

"Three years ago, the College of Anatomy was short of cadavers, especially those showing skeletal deformities."

Twist.

"The Proctor in charge of procuring specimens had just received an award for budgetary management."

Twiiist.

Phillip tried to struggle, but the chair held him fast.

"This Proctor saved money by utilizing some very unsavory sources. Gypsy grave robbers, for example."

Twist.

"I learned from one of those Gypsies, one who occupied this very chair, that they desecrated the tomb of one Tabitha MacOwen, dead before her time of a rare bone disease."

Twist

"These Gypsies sold her to this Proctor, who then had her poor wee body butchered by inept buffoons who were incapable of learning from her."

Phillip's tormentor leaned close, eyes burning with hatred, fingers tightening on the wicked machine's turn-screw.

"That Proctor's name was Phillip DeGranz."

A final violent twist of the screw, and Phillip's head exploded with pain and the horrible sensation of the two halves of his palate tearing upwards into his sinus cavity.

As his vision narrowed to a point, then went dark, Phillip just had time for one last satisfaction.

MacOwen had lost his bet after all.

CUPIDS

JASON A. ADAMS

To all those who never read the instructions.

CHAPTER 1

CASTROS BIANCHI RODE over the railroad tracks out to his menagerie, reflecting on his good fortune. He'd been in transportation his whole life, and now enjoyed using a different pre-spacing conveyance every day. Today, he sat atop a quaint steel bicycle. He'd had quite a time getting it away from the Museum of Human Travel, but the combination of credits and "friendly" overtures had finally sufficed.

After starting as a valet on Trans-Vegan Spaceways, Castros had impressed, cajoled, manipulated, and sometimes strong-armed his way onto the board. Now he was semi-retired, enjoying his own private moon orbiting the violet gas giant Vega-7, which he privately called Purple Jesus. Few people these days got the joke, mainly those in his antique cocktail club.

The old trillionaire strolled among force cages

and heavily bio-formed habitats. Past the Betelgeusan owlbears, the Terran ocelots, the Ionian rhinocrabs – a lifetime of collected species, all either near-extinct, or near-unobtainable due to distance, cost, whatever.

He excelled at getting what other people didn't have.

Coming to the last enclosure, Castros was gratified to see a large crate standing open. Obviously his new prize had been delivered. This...now *this* was a find indeed! *Cherubim cupidium*, he had decided to name it.

Ah, there was the little fellow. He chuckled, delighted at the Rafaelesque creature.

At just over one standard meter in height, the creature bore a remarkable similarity to the old paintings of Roman and Greek love deities.

Well, except for the lavender skin. And the glowing green eyes that never blinked. Those were a tad unsettling. But really, his cupid *was* cute as a button.

The cupid even had the little wings. Castros felt like a kid again, watching it flutter around the enclosure. It seemed to have some intelligence, although no one had yet been able to communicate. In fact, so far it had been completely silent, except for an occasional humming. Not really musical, but with a certain pattern. Maybe that was how it communicated.

As he watched, it began to circle the outer barrier, slowly spiraling inward. Maybe it was looking for the Regulan teddys. Not their real name, but Castros liked it because they seemed just like cute, cuddly teddy bears. There were the barbed horns, but he'd had those removed after Xavier, his manservant, nearly lost a leg. Castros really needed to hire a replacement.

The teddys were nowhere to be seen, which was odd, considering he always kept treats for them in his pocket. Castros opened the force-cage and went in, whistling and snapping his fingers. Surely the teddys would come running once they saw him.

Ah! There was Manfred, the larger of the two. Castros assumed the beast was male, but who knew with xenospecies? He had planetary zoologists to worry about such things. Pets, just like his creatures out here.

The furry teddy ignored him, which was strange. Stranger still, Manfred was trying to crawl between the roots of one of the hybrid cypress-oaks. The trees took tremendous effort to keep alive, but Castros liked alien creatures in Terran settings.

And here came his cupid. Castros sat down to watch, heedless of his ridiculously expensive genuine linen pinstripe trousers. He loved to see the ways his different creatures found to play together.

The cupid spiraled above Manfred, beginning its

eerie hum. Suddenly, it plummeted onto the teddy's back and began to—

"Great jumping Jezebels!" Castros cried out, right before being violently sick.

The cupid looked up from what remained of Manfred, its purple cheeks smeared with Manfred's green blood and clots of fur. Castros froze, unnerved by the calm appraisal. When the thing bent back to its meal, Castros ran.

CHAPTER 2

CASTROS PANTED as he dumped his bicycle and ran into the sprawling house. He had spent years and a large fortune decorating the building to look like an archaic rail terminal, but today he didn't see the timetables, vintage posters of long-gone destinations, or brass ticket windows.

He ducked into the ornate filigreed telephone booth, opening the ancient box to reveal the much more prosaic hyperlink console inside. He punched in a code long known by heart, and waited.

The screen brightened to reveal a hard, whiskered visage. The black hair framed a lean, scarred face, from which two ice-blue eyes fixed him like a laser.

"Castros," the man said, omitting any pleasantries. "What kinda shit you in now?"

"Hello, Beekman," Castros said. "I—What do you mean by that?"

"Look, Boss," Beekman said. "You and I go way back. I respect you. You always pay your people on time and as agreed. But, since you retired you've called me twice. Three times, now. Both the other calls were because you needed some dirty work done, so I ain't holding out for an invite to the beach, know what I mean?"

"Well, now," Castros said, clearing his throat as his face burned. "I consider you a valuable employee, and don't wish to disturb you without reason."

"Thanks. Whaddaya want?"

"I have a problem," Castros said, ignoring the snort fifteen light-years away. "One of my new specimens appears to be a bit more dangerous than I bargained for."

"I ain't surprised," Beekman said. "I always told you one of those things was gonna cause you trouble."

"I think it just needs some training," Castros said. "But I'm no animal handler. I want you to come and cage it for me."

"How big is it?" Beekman said. "Don't you have zookeepers?"

"I did," Castros said, rubbing his forehead. "They seem to have taken unplanned leave."

"Uh-huh."

"Look. I'll pay you double your rate."

"Okay, fine. And have a Garlaxian electro-stunner waiting."

"Done," Castros said. "Give me your ship code, and I'll upload the coordinates." He ended the link.

CHAPTER 3

THE NEXT DAY, Castros stood at the landing field, watching the approach of a sleek, black T36 Cheetah-class personal transport. The pre-programmed autopilot brought it arcing in over the green and azure forest, reflecting the purple glow of Vega-7.

The ship banked sharply, then settled its struts onto the plascrete landing pad, its atmospheric drives throwing leaves and debris in a wide arc. What a mess, he thought. But, he had servo-bots, and now he had the best bag man he knew.

"Beekman!" he called. "Welcome to my humble abode."

"Yeah, it's nice," said the squat, muscular pilot as he strode down the gangway, a heavy duffel over one shoulder. "Got any beer?"

"Well, yes," Castros said, forcing the genteel smile back on. Beekman had no appreciation at all for what Castros had built here, the shpurtz. "Come inside and I'll give you the details."

In the sprawling den, decorated with animal skins and mounted heads from over a hundred species from as many worlds, Castros told Beekman what he knew of *Cherubim cupidium*. Which wasn't much, true. Damn those miscreant handlers!

"So what you know is the thing's purple and it flies," Beekman said, polishing the electro-stunner's already gleaming business end.

"Er, yes," Castros said, tugging at his collar. "And it seems to be a vicious little bugger right now. But I'm sure it can be tamed."

"Uh-huh."

"Seriously, Beekman," he said, flushing. "That damned cupid has already cost me more than half my other specimens put together! The transport crew alone wanted three times as much as usual."

"And I'm only getting double?" Beekman said, one eyebrow rising.

"Well, we had an agreement," Castros said. When Beekman merely stared at him, Castros sighed and threw his hands up. "Fine. Triple for you too. Now go get my cupid back in its box."

"Sure thing, Boss," Beekman said with a grin. "Lead the way."

Castros took Beekman and his gun back to the enclosure, this time in a luxury speeder instead of one of his preferred vintage vehicles. In less than three minutes, they were back at the enclosure, where a door-shaped row of blinking red lights blinked redly at them.

"Oh dear," Castros said, slumping in the driver's seat.

"What now?" asked Beekman.

"I *may* have left the gate open."

"On how many cages?" Beekman asked. Castros followed his gaze toward one flashing rectangle after another.

"Surely the cupid isn't that intelligent," Castros said, hating the tremble in his voice.

"It might be the smartest thing on this rock," Beekman said under his breath.

They drove past the enclosures, Castros feeling an ache in his chest at the splashes of blood and ichor in various hues. He saw no bones or other bodily evidence, so perhaps his pets were merely wounded.

Then he saw the huge body of an owlbear lying in the swampy fen of its enclosure, its back toward them. The feathred hulk vibrated and twitched, and Castros leapt from the speeder and ran toward the force-cage's opening.

"Get back here, you idiot!" Beekman yelled.

"I'm going to save at least one of my menagerie!" Castros hollered back. "Cover me!" He'd heard that phrase in a vid from the Pre-Expansion Age.

"With what? A blanket?"

Castros ignored him.

He was a couple of meters from the owlbear when the skin near the middle of its spine swelled in two humps, as if it were growing human breasts on the wrong side. The green hide split, and two lavender heads emerged, covered in gore. Four green eyes glowed at him unblinking.

"Get down, Boss!" Beekman cried out behind him.

Castros, his knees already weak, fell to the mud as a bright bolt of energy streamed over his head, tearing into the carcass with a crackling hiss. The stench of burnt hair filled his nostrils.

Beekman ran to Castros, pulling him to his feet. "There, that knocked the little shits—"

A sharp humming like an overloaded power panel came from the body as two purplish figures shot from the gaping hole toward the cage entrance. Both men hit the ground again, arms over their heads, droplets of owlbear blood spattering down.

Beekman recovered first, jumping up and running full-tilt toward the opening.

"Beekman, damn you!" Castros said, struggling to his feet and chasing his cowardly thug. "Don't leave me in here with those…those *things!*"

"They ain't here anymore, Boss," Beekman called back over his shoulder. "But we might be if those little bastards have the gate controls figured out!"

The landscape took on a bluish cast as the moon rotated away from Vega-7 and Vega itself peeped over the horizon. Long, double shadows crept along the ground as slowly as Castros, who was doing his best to sneak back to his speeder.

Before he got there, however, the craft lurched to one side, then fell to the ground with a resounding crash. Two tiny figures shot away toward the distant trees.

"How far back to your place?" Beekman asked, scanning the spot where he'd last seen the cupids.

"About ten klicks," Castros said, mourning the fate of his custom-made boots and spats.

The two set off, jumping at every sound. The menagerie was eerily quiet. The only sounds were wind in the vegetation, Castros' panting, and Beekman's occasional curse. At least the moon had no *native* life for the cupids to murder, Castros thought.

CHAPTER 4

THEY MADE IT BACK TO CASTROS' home without incident, and immediately went through the entire place, securing every opening to the outside. Since installing the habitat and cloaking sphere around the entire planetoid, Castros tended to leave his windows open so he could hear his pets out in the menagerie. Now he wished he had battlecruiser plates for shutters.

"What shall we do now?" he asked Beekman, who was laying out bits of machinery from his duffle.

"Now we forget stunning your toys, and take the assholes out," Beekman replied, assembling all the flotsam into a wicked-looking pulse rifle.

"You mean *kill* them?" Castros gawped at Beekman, wondering how the man could be so cruel.

"They're just following their instincts. We can't hold dumb beasts responsible for their actions."

Beekman stared at Castros, mouth hanging open. "Are you serious, Boss? Those 'dumb beasts' figured out how to open all your cages and disable your speeder. Who knows what else they can figure out?"

"Yes, true, but—"

"But nothin'," Beekman said. "This ain't a dog catcher situation any more. You can get one of your brainiac xenologists or whatever you call your pet science guys down here. I'm gone."

"You can't leave now," Castros said, some of the take-no-prisoners steel from his days as master of one of the galaxy's largest teamster organizations back in his voice. "I'll not pay you a drop if you do."

"Shove your money." Beekman stood and looped the gun's sling over his shoulder. "Dead men can't spend anything." He walked to the door, punching the button and waiting while it hissed open.

"Surely we can come to an agreement," Castros said.

"Surely we can," Beekman said. He still stood at the open door. Then he pushed the button again.

He turned back to Castros with empty eyes. "Every panel on my ship is laying on the ground, along with most of the wiring. The door to your hangar is open too."

"Oh dear," Castros said.

"Screw it," Beekman said. "I'm calling some of the boys." He pulled out a pocket comm unit, twiddled the screen and dials, then swore loudly and threw it across the room.

"No signal," Beekman said. "How about you?"

Castros went to the phone booth, unsurprised when the screen remained blank. He went from room to room, reliably disappointed every time he tried a comm unit.

"No soap," he said. "The vids are out as well. The entire comm array must be down."

"That's great. That's ab-so-lutely *stellar!*" Beekman shouted, stomping around the room, sending several priceless curios to smash on the floor and walls. "How long until someone shows up? Deliveries? Guests?"

"Um," Castros said sheepishly. "Never. Only a few people know about this moon, and none of them have coordinates. I always upload an encrypted autonav package to their vessels personally. I value my privacy." He knew he shouldn't defend himself to an employee, but was regretting his lack of a social life.

"Please tell me you're shitting me," Beekman said, hard eyes glittering.

"Look, let's not bicker," Castros said, doing his best to be reasonable. "We need to fix the array."

"You know how?"

"Of course I do," Castros said indignantly.

He hoped so, anyway.

But when they stepped outside, they saw at least seven small lavender figures buzzing around the compound. Even worse, all the creatures stopped as soon as Castros and Beekman began edging toward the comm array, and soon spiraled directly over their heads. The whir of their wings and the constant humming set Castros' teeth on edge.

"Think we can get back inside?" Beekman asked.

"We have to fix the antennae," Castros replied.

"You know," Beekman said. "It occurs to me that maybe they'll leave me alone if there's other grub handy."

Castros stopped short, turning to see Beekman cradling his pulse rifle. His eyes were cold, calculating.

"What are you saying?" Castros said, ice running down his spine. "I hope not what I think."

"You've been a good boss up 'til now," Beekman said, raising the rifle. "But I ain't ready to feed the animals. Know what I mean?"

"I'll pay you four times what we agreed," Castros said, raising his arms to his face. "Five times!"

"Your money's no good here," Beekman said without emotion. "I'm sorry, Boss. I—"

Castros nearly fainted when Beekman screamed. Warm liquid ran down his trouser leg as pulse rifle fire throbbed in a wide arc, missing Castros but blowing holes in the base of the gleaming comm array.

Castros peeked through his fingers when the noise stopped. A mound of cupids hummed over the humped shape of his ex-employee. Castros gulped convulsively, then spotted the pulse rifle on the ground, not a meter from him.

"Okay, you foul shpurtzers," he whispered. "Okay, you worthless bags of shit."

He crept forward and leaned down, never taking his eyes from the rapidly diminishing mound.

"That's right, keep eating."

He had the rifle now, slowly raising it toward the heap of meat and cupids.

"Just stay still a few more seconds…"

A high-pitched humming dropped from the sky behind Castros, and the back of his expensive trousers filled.

"Oh dear."

CHAPTER 5

"READY TO OPEN THE GATE?" Lamont Stevenson asked.

"Ready to go, sir," Hendricks answered.

The two stood in a large laboratory on Betelgeuse Station, insulated from the surrounding klicks of hubbub by heavily soundproofed plasteel. It would not do for any curious citizens to come in just now.

"Are you positive you're locked onto Bianchi's Moon?" said Stevenson.

"One hundred percent, sir," Hendricks said, voice full of confident pride. "My research over the last five years is conclusive. The second moon of Vega-7."

"Wonderful!" Stevenson said, rubbing his hands and chuckling.

The private hideout of one of the galaxy's

richest men, lost for nearly seventy-five years. If the rumors about Bianchi's collections were true, Stevenson and Hendricks would soon be buying their own moons.

"Open 'er up!" Stevenson shouted, eyes fixed on the portal framework. Hendricks' fingers danced on his keypad, a violet plasma filled the space between the uprights, and a hole onto another world opened.

A decade ago, portal technology had taken a massive leap. What was once only good for opening wormholes for spacecraft had been wrangled down until a gate only a couple of meters wide could be opened. Not just in empty space, either. The new technology led to a new breed of detectives and collectors.

Or thieving salvagers. Whatever.

He was soon going to be wealthy beyond the most vile dreams of avarice.

The space on the other side of the portal was filled with strange plant life. Stevenson thought he recognized the green and brown stuff from historical vids of ancient Earth, but he also saw other plants in every color of the spectrum. Neat.

Hendricks helped Stevenson with his biosuit, and Stevenson returned the favor. No one knew exactly what had happened to the eccentric old collector, but alien microbes or some other disease was a good bet. Even his enemies among the transport guilds claimed innocence, and that crowd was usually only too happy to boast.

Hendricks locked the console, ensuring the portal would stay open until they returned, and he followed Stevenson onto the distant moon's surface.

They came through only a half-klick from a low compound of buildings, overgrown with vines and underbrush. Their external suit mikes picked up nothing but the lonely sound of wind in the leaves.

"Good job, Hendricks!" Stevenson said, clapping him on the shoulder.

"We got lucky," Hendricks said nonchalantly. "Let's go check it out. I think I see an old racing ship!"

They walked as quickly as the bulky suits allowed, past the remnants of long-dead force-cages, until they reached what appeared to be the main structure.

"Think this is it?" Hendricks asked. The odd, vine-covered building didn't look like any house he'd ever seen. Man-tall arched windows covered the sides. Deep eaves cast shade along the entire length. But a large painted sign declared this "Bianchi Depot," so that pretty much settled it.

"Must be," Stevenson said, looking around at all the bizarre decorations. "He sure liked his dead animals, didn't he?"

"See what you can find in there," Hendricks said. "I want to see if the ship is salvageable. I know a guy who restores classics. He might give us a pretty good chunk for it."

"Sounds good," Stevenson said, stepping through the open door. He tried the light panel, with no luck. The power probably died decades ago. Plenty of light streamed through the large windows, enough for him to see…

Nothing. Nothing was out of place, except the debris you'd expect after so many years of wind-blown detritus. Through a window on the left, he saw a large communications structure, scarred and pitted along the base. Maybe signs of violence, maybe just signs of neglect.

While he searched room by room, a faint humming filled the suit speakers. He tapped the side of his helmet, and was rewarded with a shrill electronic squawk, and then silence.

The annoying hum started up again.

"Hendricks, are you hearing all that noise?" he said, looking around for the source.

The humming grew steadily louder.

"Hendricks?"

TO CATCH
A THIEF

An Appalachian Gothic Tale

JASON A. ADAMS
Author of *Mick of Malvern* and *Sunlit Dispositions*

In loving memory of Granny Pearlie.

CHAPTER 1

SOMETIMES AN OLD DOG'S nose is the only warning we get of the weird critters that seep through the walls of this world.

Larry's great-granny had taught him that before he could look across her battered old kitchen table without being up on his toes. The old herb woman been full of lessons *her* granny had brought over from the old country, stories of other times and places, and of the magic that grew right up out of the lush earth. You could feel it in the woods, she said. You could listen and hear the wind and the trees layin' their plans.

Larry used to love hearing her old voice drawin' them other worlds down, sitting in one of the dark bentwood rockers while she twisted her cobweb hair up into its screaming bun, the air thick and hot and heavy as an old dowry quilt fresh from the washbucket. The critters, the normal critters, would be a-singin' the summer to bed as the days got shorter and the temperature still soared.

Granny Pearlie's old homeplace was a small but sturdy tin-roofed cabin, the foot-thick chestnut logs telling their own story of great forests gone by, and the wraparound porch of splintery pine boards would catch the evening breeze. To Larry, that breeze always sounded like it was commentin' on the tales, like it knew more than the ignorant dirt scratchers of Dickenson County.

Larry wished she was still around now. He sure could use her advice.

CHAPTER 2

LARRY CRABTREE HAD BEEN sheriff of Dickenson County for the last ten years. In all that time, he'd no more to deal with than teenage hooliganism, family squabbles, getting drunks off the road—the usual small town stuff. Oh, there was the occasional dead body, whether from a highway wreck or by their own hand, but Holly Creek was a quiet town. Mostly.

This, though. This was getting a mite weird. Abry Stanley's cows had been getting sick over the last year, withering away or else giving milk that was clabbered and streaked with blood and pus. His youngest, twelve-year-old Cathy, was also feeling puny. Just getting weaker and more pale, day by day. She was really his granddaughter. Her daddy dead in the mines, and her mamma run off doing who knew what, who knew where. Abe had taken in the two little'uns, and did his best by them, but Cathy wasn't doing well at all.

Seemed like there was always one or two girls in Bonnie Skeens' seventh grade classes with the same ailment, and this year was poor Cathy's turn. Doc Phipps didn't know what to do for them, and every test came back negative. Physically, Cathy was healthy as a horse. No reason for it. Like she was pinin' to death like someone in those old romance stories.

CHAPTER 3

LARRY WASN'T THINKING a bit about Abry and his problems as he walked up Main Street to the courthouse and his small office behind. The mid-September breeze was cool this morning, hinting at colder weather on the way. On the ridges, the maples and oaks were wearing their party colors of red, yellow, and orange, prettying themselves up for one last hoorah before bedding down for the winter.

He waved and passed a word with the townies he met, most of them faces he'd known all his life. Or their lives in the case of the younger, of which there were more and more as he grew increasingly vintage. The town was awake, the daily rounds of the old brick and wood businesses well underway. Most of the buildings in what passed for a downtown dated back fifty years or more, to the times of coal and lumber booms. The mines and mills were mostly gone now, but the town stayed alive and the people endured.

Old Mrs. Carter grabbed him for a few minutes of bellyaching about the noise from Dana's place. She was swelled up and had high color under the paint on her cheeks. Dana kept a pack of beagles that he called huntin' dogs, and everyone else called spoiled troublemakers. They'd gotten out of the fence again and trampled her prized violet patch and didn't he know how much time and love she put into her garden and Lord why couldn't he keep them mutts under control. Larry promised to talk to Dana again, more to get away from her than because he thought it would do any good.

The County school bus roared by, delivering the daily load to the high school. Old Sheila Powers behind the wheel, waving as she passed. Miz Sheila she'd been to him since he first rode the clanky old thing, almost four decades ago. She'll outlive us all, he thought as he entered the old brick building he shared with the Commonwealth Attorney and other magisterials. Miz Sheila had to be well in her seventies, but was still spry and sassy as a woman half her age. Didn't look a day over fifty, but that might be the hair dye and layers of makeup. He didn't think she'd had any work done, not on her pay. Maybe she just got lucky in the gene lottery.

He greeted Pauline, the young receptionist who'd been riding Miz Sheila's bus just a couple of years ago, picked up his mail and memos, then stepped into his office to see Abry standing there.

Abry had his old hat in his hands, wringing it tightly, nervous as a bug. His grey hair bristled in the angry crewcut he'd probably been born with, and his eyes were haunted, darting around the office before lighting on Larry's.

"The Devil's come to my house Larry," he said, serious as could be. Larry, who'd seen more of the world than the Virginia coalfields after a few years in the Army, had gotten over most of the superstitions and backwood beliefs of his raising. But he knew better than to outright scoff at such declarations. Folks got ugly when you made out they were being foolish.

So he told the old farmer to park himself in the chair opposite. Pauline came in with coffee for them both. Abry didn't even look at his. Just shuffled his booted feet, squirming in the heavy wooden chair, hands tucked in the flaps of his worn biballs.

"What makes you think that, Abe?" Larry finally asked. "Seen a big red feller with a hayfork?" He was trying to get a smile out of Abry, get him to relax a little, but no luck there.

"Nossir. Nothin' like that." Abry leaned forward and looked Larry right in the eye. "You ever see a big black critter, big as an ol' papa bear? But not no bear, and not anything I ever seen before. Kinda like a big panther, but shaped wrong, somehow. Dint have no legs that I could see, but still moved like a cat."

"Come on, Abe. There ain't any panthers left—"

"I seen that thing sniffin' around outside Cathy's bedroom door," Abry said. "Inside the house. I never heard nothin' until I seen it in the hall." His hands were again twisting and wringing in his lap. "I hollered, you bet I did. It looked right at me, give out a high lonesome wail, like a widder woman at her man's funeral. It shot past me and jumped out the hall winder. I run to look, but it was gone, just like that. The dogs was all hollerin' fit to split, and like to never calmed down."

He looked hard at Larry, like he was trying to make him believe just by force of will. "That winder's on the downslope side of the house. Thirty foot or more off the ground. I went outside and hunted, but nary a print nor nothin' did I see. Only thing left of it was its stink, like dirty coal smoke fulla sulphur. The worst of it, though…when that… whatever it was…looked at me, it looked at me with a human bein's eyes. Blue, like a deep lake, and fulla hate."

Larry leaned back and considered. He figured Abry had seen something all right, probably a 'coon had snuck in and then got spooked and climbed out the window and down the wall. But a mountain lion? They'd been hunted to death close on a hundred years ago. He figured old Abe had been half asleep or half snockered and let his imagination get away with him.

"Well Abry, I can get hold of the game warden, see if he'll come over and set a trap or two. Would that do ya?"

"I'm goin' to ketch that thing tonight, Sheriff," Abry said. "I don't know what it is, or what all it's a-doin', but I don't mean to let it have another try at my Cathy." He stood and turned toward the door, then looked back. "Can you come, Larry? Tonight? My mind's set and I'll not change it, but I sure wouldn't say no to some comp'ny."

Larry meant to say no, to tell Abry that it wasn't anything but some wild critter snuck in his house, but the old man was giving him a look that said I ain't gonna beg, but I'm begging all the same. Larry heaved a deep breath, trying to disguise a sigh.

"Okay, Abe. I'll meet you at your place around nine tonight."

CHAPTER 4

LARRY FELT A FOOL. What in the world was he doing out in Abry's field at three in the morning? He'd let the worried farmer talk him into standing watch, but enough was enough. He was cold, hungry, and plumb tuckered.

He stood, meaning to tell Abry they should call it a night, when his companion grabbed his elbow and yanked him down.

"There! Just by the barn. That's the same damn thing!" Abry's eyes had gone wide and his hand shook a little on Larry's arm, but when he let go and pulled his old hunting rifle around, he brought it up steady as a rock. His hound dogs had started up their alarm, barking like crazy.

The sheriff could see a massive black form coming from the trees toward the barn. He couldn't make out what the thing was. It was...*smudged* came to mind. Indistinct. But the shape was *wrong*, somehow. It seemed upright, but he saw no limbs or head. He blinked, doubting his eyes when he saw the thing's shadow leading it, between its body and the light from the house.

Like the shadow was casting the figure.

The hairs on his neck and arms stood straight up. It was definitely not one of Abry's livestock. Slowly, almost oozing along, it seeped toward the barn, making no noise he could hear. Not over Abry's dogs, anyhow.

Just outside the door it stopped, raised up, and slowly turned, a distinct snuffling sound reaching Larry's ears, until it was facing them. Larry saw it freeze, going on point he could tell, and heard the distant ethereal keening Abry had told of.

"Get it!" Abry hollered, and started firing his .30-06 as fast as he could work the bolt.

Larry wasn't far behind, jacking shells and pulling the trigger until the shotgun ran dry. God help him, he'd seen a person's blue eyes in that black and misshapen face, boring straight into his own. Those eyes stood out in the night like he was right there in front of the thing, not on a hill over forty yards away.

The beast turned and fled toward the treeline, flowing across the pasture like an undulate hole in the world. It was making a noise that Larry would remember the rest of his life. A howling, cackling laugh. A laugh full of evil and cunning and mockery. But a human laugh just the same.

"Sweetjesuslordgodamighty," Abry said, eyes bigger than saucers, shaking like a leaf. "What the hell is it, Larry?"

"I don't have a clue, Abe," he said. "But I don't think Jesus has anything to do with it." He left Abry standing watch and went back to his cruiser for an extra flashlight. When he returned, the grizzled and frazzled farmer was in exactly the same position, eyes still wide and staring.

The two of them walked slowly toward the barn, heavy six-cell Maglites sweeping over the grass, the barn, and out toward the trees.

Nothing. No tracks, no crushed blades of grass, no stains—nothing but a faint reek of rancid cabbage or spoiled eggs.

Brimstone.

Larry glanced in the barn to check the animals. The cows were frantic, lowing and stomping, but they didn't seem hurt. Even Abry's prize milker Strawberry didn't look any worse. No better, either, but she'd been down for over a month. It struck Larry then that the dogs had gone quiet.

Abry looked his stock over, forked some sweet hay into their troughs to soothe them, then the two men spent nearly three hours going over every inch of the pasture between the house and the woods, in line with the barn and about fifty yards to either side. Nothing at all. Even the smell was gone by the time Larry called a halt.

"Abe, I don't reckon that sucker will be back today, not with dawn coming up. I doubt it'll try anything when it ain't dark. Besides, I can't take much more tonight, and you don't look any better." He rose, shook Abry's hand, and turned down the hill. "You call me if your dogs so much as squeak again and I'll come runnin', but for now I'll be at the old home place. I got to think on this."

CHAPTER 5

THE OLD HOME place was his granny's house, where he'd lived since his Army stint was up. He still loved the place, with its memories and hints of the old woman who'd half raised him.

Larry would swear he could still feel her, like her spirit had soaked into the beams and logs. Even her old table still stood in the kitchen, the table he'd helped make many a meal at. She'd taught him about cooking, lore, and life in general until she finally passed at close on a hundred years old. He'd been twenty then. Nearly thirty years ago, and he missed that old bird yet.

He paced around the four small rooms, listening to the plain but tough heartwood pine creaking under his feet, trying to sort out what all he and Abry'd seen and heard. Finally, exhaustion—physical, mental, and emotional—took him as the first purple glow swelled over the mountains to the east. He barely got out of his uniform before crashing across his huge feathertick mattress in the back bedroom.

CHAPTER 6

IN HIS DREAMS, he was back at Abry's but far too close to the barn. Something gigantic and black was coming for him, eyes blazing out of the darkness. He couldn't run, couldn't shout, couldn't do anything but wait as ice started to build on his skin and in his hair.

It knew him.

It wanted him.

It would not let him interfere.

The dark folds rolled over him and he fell...

Suddenly the dream changed. No swirling mist, no sense of motion, but here he was standing in Granny's kitchen, and everything was too big. He looked down at himself and saw the knee-torn blue jeans, the scuffed Keds, the small arms and hands. This was the kitchen as he remembered it when

Granny was alive, and he'd become the boy that stored the memory.

Warm yellow light came through the windows, lighting up the floating dust, turning every sunbeam into a dancing Milky Way. Morning sun, he thought. The sun's just out of bed.

"That's right," the old familiar voice said. "Daybreak and day's end. The world's thinnest then. 'Specially on the cusp days."

He turned, and saw his Granny standing beside the ancient white iron and porcelain sink, kneading a huge pile of what had to be biscuit dough. His mouth watered. He hadn't had a proper cat's head biscuit since she passed.

The man was gone, and only the boy was left.

"What's a cusp day, Granny?"

"Them's the old high days, Lar-Bear. The days when the world turns. Solstice days, when the light or dark is strongest, and the days in spring and fall when they break even." She rolled out the dough and began cutting the biscuits, letting Larry have a small pinch. He held it on his tongue while she talked, feeling the tingle of the soda and tasting the raw fresh buttermilk.

"Gotta let 'em set for a bit," Granny said as she wiped her hands on an old flour sack rag. "Now we need to talk, you and me. Hop on up in a chair." She sat herself, packing her old cob pipe. Larry duly hopped, his chin just over the table's edge and his feet kicking idly above the floor.

"You got yourself a problem, Lar-Bear." She held a broomstraw to a hole in the ancient wood cookstove and lit the pipe, puffing out great clouds of blue smoke until it burned to her satisfaction, then pointed first to Larry, then to the window with the pipe stem. "You ain't chasin' a normal varmint. Guns 'n traps might as well be cornshucks for all the good they'll do."

"What was it Granny? I ain't never seen the like before."

"And you didn't see what you think you did, neither. That weren't no more than a glamour, a mask it used to hide itself from the real world." She stood and popped the tray of puffy biscuit dough into the hot oven.

"There ain't no real word for something like that. It's what you get when you mix yourself with the darkness come alive." She came around the table and sat beside Larry, tapping his knee with her bony finger. "I know you don't believe in the boogeyman no more, you're all growed up and too sensible for all that nonsense. But there's a bad soul somewhere close that's done invited the darkness into herself, tradin' with it for somethin'. Might be power, might be love, might be youth." She smiled crookedly at him, and even dropped a wink. "Just because you don't believe something, that don't mean it ain't real just the same, Lar-Bear."

"It's a thief, boy. Pure and simple. Two thieves, really. You got a human bein' stealin' one thing, and the blackness that rides the person is stealin' something else. But in the end, they're both stealin' life. If you don't do what I tell you, it'll steal all of young Cathy's life and there you'll be."

Granny pulled him to his feet and wrapped her arms around him. "Now you listen to me, Lar-Bear. It takes a thief to catch a thief. I'll tell you how to do it, but it's all up to you after that. It'll be ugly, but there ain't nothing purty about business like this."

The old woman began to talk, and Larry listened.

CHAPTER 7

LARRY CREPT from the woods to Abry's battered old chestnut log barn just after he'd seen the family help poor Cathy to the truck, likely heading to Doc Phipps's. The kid was pale as a sheet, and shuffled along like a dried out old lady instead of a young'un not even in her teens.

He wasn't quite sure why the hell he was here. It was only a dream, dammit! Yet here he was.

Wincing as the rusty tire strap hinges squealed, Larry slowly pulled the door open just enough to slip through. Once inside, he gagged as a horrid stink slid up his nostrils and down the back of his throat. He barely kept his last meal down and nearly dropped the plastic tub and flashlight.

He'd been in plenty of barns and livestock pens, and never found the odors of feed, fur, and feces all that pleasant. But at least the scent of hay and the stench of manure were normal. Raw materials and finished products. Not this time, though.

The air in here was a miasmic concoction of sour milk, stale urine, and infection. The hay and manure were there as well, and the combined assault on his senses had him coughing and wiping his sleeve across his eyes inside two steps. Best be done as soon as he could.

Larry blinked, squinting through his tears as he swept the flashlight over the three small stalls. In spite of the afternoon sun streaming through the four high windows of the tiny barn, he still struggled to see into the dark recesses.

There wasn't hardly any sound, especially as he was breathing as little as possible. But he finally heard poor Strawberry wheezing in the third and rearmost stall. He stepped toward her, grateful that Abry always kept a tidy barn with no tools, tack, or fodder bales to trip over.

The hapless cow lay on her side, ribs and hip bones standing out sharply. Larry considered just putting a bullet in the poor thing's head, but couldn't.

Steal what's bein' stole, Lar-Bear. Somethin' from every sick thing at the place. That was what Granny Pearlie had said in the dream. *Get what carries the life it's after. Milk from the cow, maiden's blood from the child. She'll be having her monthlies now, that's what drew the darkness.*

This is crazy, he thought, setting the Tupperware container next to Strawberry's blotchy udder. Bruised sores covered her teats, and she gave off heat like a furnace.

Larry was years out of practice, but he still remembered how to draw milk. Only it wasn't milk he drew. It was a foul concoction of clabbered curds and pus, streaked with blood and flecks of God only knows. He got as much as he could, snapped the lid on, and ran for the door.

He just made it outside before breakfast came back in a rush.

Trembling and weak, Larry wiped his mouth and stumbled up to the house. Like most local folks, Abry didn't lock his doors, making it easy for Larry to break another law.

He crept through the house, listening for the rattle and roar of the beat-up Chevy coming back, flinching at every creak and crack from the floor. Some sheriff. This wasn't upholding the law. But he hoped it was protecting and serving the community, at least.

In the upstairs bathroom trash, Larry found the second item he needed. A tissue-wrapped menstrual pad, spotted with the roses of Cathy's approaching womanhood. He felt like a dirty and twisted old man as he dropped the pad in the goop from the barn. One more thing to get.

He found it in Ada Stanley's sewing nook. A brand new pack of needles, still in the plastic. At least he wouldn't have to steal them from a store. Time to test what he remembered.

CHAPTER 8

BACK IN HIS OFFICE, Larry shut the door and pulled the blinds. He dumped the water from his kettle and poured in the mess he'd brought from the farm. Last, he tore open the pack of needles and shook them into the pot and put the pot on the hotplate he kept for coffee and lunches. He opened the window, trying to let in some clean air.

As the coil began to glow, Larry noticed movement outside. He looked out, and his neck hairs started to dance again.

The sidewalk below his window was filling with dogs. A dozen or more already, and more coming down the street. Hound dogs. Shepherd dogs. Dana's beagles. Homeless mutts. Dogs of every breed and no breed. They came and either sat or paced, but all looked toward the road. Not toward the window. It wasn't the foulness from his kettle they were smelling.

It's the magic, he thought. That's what called them.

A reek of boiled rankness was rising from the kettle. He heard the contents bubbling, then heard an enormous crash of metal and masonry from down the street. He looked that way and saw Miz Sheila's bus had plowed into the Kendrick General Store.

Car alarms brayed. People screamed. Someone in the bus howled in agony.

The dogs just watched.

Out the back door of the bus Miz Sheila hurtled, her chin and torso covered with blood.

He thought it was all from the gash on her forehead, but as he watched she vomited a great scarlet gout, not slowing as she ran shrieking toward his office, blue eyes blazing in her too-young face.

Sheila never made it. Judging from the stain growing in her slacks, she was pouring her life's blood from both ends.

She slowed, stumbled, and fell. Finally, she stopped twitching and lay silent.

The dogs began trotting toward her still form.

By then, Larry was running himself. What the hell happened? But he knew. Miz Sheila, the beloved driver of children since his own childhood...

He got there in time to smell the stench of urine and feces added to coppery blood as her body relaxed completely, letting bladder and sphincter go. Dead, just like that.

He started to wave people back as an ambulance came wailing up from the Rescue Squad depot.

Larry was nearly knocked over as the crowd of dogs bounded past him toward Sheila's body.

She was moving. Arching her back somehow. Mouth gaping as a shimmering haze breathed out of her.

Barking and growling were the only sounds apart from the siren. The people stood with mouths hanging open as the dead woman continued to exhale.

A big German shepherd, one of Deputy Foyle's, jumped over Sheila and snapped at the wavy air.

Another dog, a stray redbone hound nearly as tall, snapped almost nose to nose with the first.

Together they worried the seemingly empty air until Larry heard something tear, like old blue jeans ripping in the seat.

There was a split second when Larry heard that keening again, loud enough to make everyone clap hands to ears, then everything went stone quiet.

The crowd on the street was frozen.

The dogs sniffed noses for a minute, then the whole pack began to scatter, walking or trotting back where they'd come from, not a care in the world.

CHAPTER 9

A WEEK LATER, Larry loafed in the soft grass beside Granny Pearlie's grave looking at a wreath of holly and hawthorn he'd hung over her rough sandstone marker.

Green and red, he thought. Colors of death, colors of new life. She'd like that.

The seasons roll on.

Abry had come to see him that morning. They still had a ways to travel yet, but Cathy and Strawberry were both on the mend.

"Like night 'n day," Abe had said, then shuffled his feet and stuck out his hand.

"I knowed your Granny. Know what she done fer folks. She was a fine woman, and you're a fine man. You done her right proud."

Larry shook with him, touched, something stinging at his eyes, at a loss for words. He knew

Miss Skeens' seventh-grade girls wouldn't be getting sick anymore.

Granny Pearlie was in the small plot up the hill from the old home place, along with a slew of other Crabtree relatives. He thought about the old woman, her lessons of long ago, and the more recent ones as well. This past week had led to a powerful shift in him, the letting go of so much knowing and his rediscovery of believing.

He thought on Miz Sheila and how you never can tell what hides behind a face.

The autopsy report just said "esophageal perforation." Doc Phipps told him privately it looked like she'd swallowed a porcupine.

Larry knew the real cause. Yes he did. And that was something he needed to think on as well.

Time to go clean out Granny's attic and see what-all of her things were still there.

He stood, wiped his seat, and called over to the rangy redbone hound busily anointing the headstones of his ancestors, a new friend he'd picked up after all the excitement.

"Come on Skinner, time to go home."

MALAYA

JASON A. ADAMS

To all the women who won't put up with it.

CHAPTER 1

THE LOUD CRACKLE as Billy Holbrook stretched backward was the sound of hard work well done. Almost half a cord of good hardwood split and stacked today, and the sun still high. Old Man Winter wouldn't be able to get in the house this year, that's for sure. His trick knee was just now starting to warn him. The doc was right about those stretches and exercises. Pro football wasn't in his future, but the knee got better all the time.

All around the odd, shedlike house, everything was making ready for the long cold ahead. A couple of cardinals swooped by, the male already dressed in his scarlet coat. Squirrels crashed through the undergrowth, sounding a hundred times their size as they scampered through the dry leaves on the forest floor. A couple of foxes were too busy with their own wrestling to bother with the squirrels.

Billy's family had lived here long enough that the humans were just another part of the landscape. His uncle had built this house on the ruins of the old family cabin. The house was a dark tan cube, the walls built of naturally aged hemlock planks and rising straight up nearly thirty feet to the sloping tin roof. A hundred and fifty years or more of Holbrook sweat was soaked into this mountain, and the woods were as much a part of his home as he was of them.

Billy glanced over his ongoing preparations with pride. Three full cords of wood, with the fourth taking shape. Heavy wooden shutters ready to close out the harsh winds that sometimes ran down the valley. Shelves full of grain, oats, beans – all the dry goods that would get them by if the road got snowed under.

He hoped that wouldn't happen.

Malaya walked past, carrying an armload of smaller kindling. At barely five feet tall and ninety pounds wringing wet, she couldn't manage the axe very well. But she'd found his granddad's old bolo machete in the shed, and that suited her just fine. With the gray dungarees and heavy work shirts she usually wore, the machete looked made for her. Her silver bracelets, heavy and inlaid with cinnabar designs, somehow didn't look out of place with the work clothes.

Billy had never known just what her real background was. He'd met her at Clark Air Base in the Philippines, and they'd taken to each other well enough. Malaya hopped tables at the NCO Club in the evenings. During the day, she was involved with some student organization out there, but didn't talk about it. She was a tough little bird though, and Billy had some notions about how she'd gotten so good with a jungle knife.

They'd dated for a few months. Billy met her family, or at least the women and girls. Mal said her daddy and a couple of brothers were still alive, just not home much. Working, she said, but never where or how.

A traffic accident had cut Billy's enlistment short. Some young kid in a jeep that didn't know how slick Filipino mud could be during the rainy season. The jeep had slid off the road, coming straight for Billy, who jumped out of the way.

And landed wrong, tearing a bunch of tendons and cartilage in his right knee. What a heroic way to end his military career.

Once the doc said he'd be a medical, Billy had asked Malaya to come home with him. He was pretty sure he loved her, even though he didn't know much about her or what she did when they weren't together. She'd kissed him, said she would, and had him in front of a priest a few days later.

And now, here they were. Most of his family

accepted his Asian wife, and most of the folks out to town were friendly enough.

Most.

He just wished they wouldn't start talking louder and slower whenever they spoke to Mal. She might have an accent, but she spoke English just fine. Along with Spanish, Tagalog, Japanese, and Chinese.

Hell, Billy wouldn't be surprised if aliens landed and she started chatting with them in Martian.

As he watched her glide back toward the woodlot, making almost no noise in spite of the leaf-littered ground, he again wondered if bringing her home to Virginia had been a good idea. The people in town were a little scared of her, probably just because of her Asian features and strange accent.

To be honest, sometimes Billy was a little scared of her too.

The way he sometimes caught her staring at him, her often-expressionless face and dark, dark eyes giving nothing away. The odd assortment of statues, beads, and other artifacts she'd insisted on keeping weren't very comforting either.

A loud, shrill cry came from the woodlot. Not Malaya's voice, something animal. Billy wondered what she'd killed this time.

Deer, as it turned out. Brained it with the machete.

How the hell had she gotten close enough to the doe to manage that?

Billy decided not to ask questions. He thunked the axe down into his splitting stump and went to help Malaya dress her kill.

CHAPTER 2

A COUPLE OF HOURS LATER, he and Malaya headed to town in Billy's beat-up old Chevy truck. His shoulders still ached a little from swinging the axe half the morning, but Malaya had rubbed most of the pain out, her silver bracelets tinkling, soothing his ears while she soothed his muscles. For a tiny little thing, she had strong hands.

Shame she couldn't do the same for his trick knee.

"What all you want with your deer steak?" he asked Malaya as they went down the curvy road. "Salad? Corn?"

She shrugged. "I make *pancit palabok*, if you like."

Shrimp noodles. Billy loved them. Malaya made the dish a couple of times a month and he always ate too much.

"Sounds great, Mal." Billy said. He hoped the Piggly Wiggly had some rice noodles. It just wasn't the same with spaghetti.

CHAPTER 3

THEY PULLED into the Pig's parking lot, which was packed. So was the liquor store next door.

Shit. Billy hadn't thought. First Friday of the month. Paycheck day and food stamp day. Easy to forget when the magic of direct deposit kept up with his VA money and settlement pay.

Billy winced at all the hate-filled bumper stickers and window decals. Strange how people could be friendly as can be, while still being hateful as hell toward most folks on the planet.

"You okay with this, Mal?" he asked, turning the key and waiting as the truck coughed and grumbled itself to sleep. Maybe they should've stayed home so he could clean the carburetor.

Malaya cocked her head and looked at him, almost smiling.

"I be okay, honey. So will you. Come, let us get done and get home."

She opened the door and jumped out, landing without a sound, and started toward the store with her back straight and head held high. The setting sun sparked fire from her bracelets, spots of light dancing over the cars she walked past.

Damn. Billy couldn't let her go in there alone.

What kind of husband would that make him?

He stepped out and caught up with Malaya easily enough. She took his hand and gave it a squeeze.

The automatic doors whooshed open and they went in. Billy's gut clenched when the roar of a hundred conversations died. Every face turned their way, and most whipped back to something else.

He could feel their desire to stare though. Felt his anger and impatience with the home folks.

Reminded himself that most of them never got further from home than Gatlinburg or Myrtle Beach.

Miz Skeens, his old English teacher stopped on her way out, buggy loaded down with groceries.

"Hello William," she said, beaming at him before she turned to Malaya.

"And-how-are-you, Mrs.-Holbrook?" she said, voice going up a couple-dozen decibels and slowing down to a crawl.

Malaya muttered something under her breath.

Billy'd never picked up much Filipino, but it sounded like something that would start a fight.

"I am very fine, ma'am," Malaya said, speaking softly. "Are your ears troubling you? I have a medicine—"

Billy took Malaya's arm. "Mighty fine to see you, Miz Skeens, but we gotta get in there before the store's wiped plumb clean."

Miz Skeens Didn't mean anything by it, Billy knew. She only meant to be friendly. But dang, Mal was family now, and had been here for over a year. Why couldn't people pay attention?

They went up one aisle and down the next, Malaya driving the buggy while Billy did the reaching up and stooping down. Worcestershire sauce and Cajun rub for the venison, fish sauce and rice noodles for the palabok.

People greeted Billy, some remembered Mal. All followed him and his strange looking wife with their eyes. Billy could feel it.

But no one said anything ugly.

Billy smiled and nodded, nodded and smiled.

They were walking past the beer cooler when it happened.

"Why, hell. If it ain't Billy and Missus Horblook!"

Dammit. Billy turned around and saw Silas Fleming and his brother Al. Both within a year or two of Billy's own age, both dressed and acting like teenagers. T-shirts with the sleeves ripped off, faded jeans with the knees torn out, all topped with greasy mullets. A perfect pair to match the thirty-year-old blood-red Camaro that was Si's pride and joy.

"You forget how to say Holbrook?" Billy said, stepping in front of Malaya.

"That's how chinks say it, ain't it?" Al said. He grinned, showing off ragged, blackened stumps instead of teeth.

"I say *Holbrook*," Mal said. "I can perhaps teach you how to say correctly. And I am not Chinese, so am not a *chink*."

"Damn, Al," Si said, elbowing his younger brother. "She can talk English and everything. Didn't know you could teach a chink—"

"Shut yer goddamn pie hole, Fleming," Billy said, hands clenching into fists. "You treat my wife with respect, you hear me?"

"Or what," Al said, sneering. "You'll run off again? Just like you always done in school? Like when you went in the Air Force?"

Howard Blevins, the store manager, came hurrying over just as Billy shoved Al hard, a display of paper plates tumbling down around them.

Billy turned toward Si, fists raised, and...

Felt his knee go.

No pain, not yet.

But his right leg folded under him and Billy continued his spin all the way down.

"You boys knock that off!" Howard yelled. His face burned red as an overheated wood stove and sweat marked the pits of his white oxford shirt. "Go on, get out of here. I've called the police, they'll be here in a couple of minutes. If you're still here, I'll press charges!"

"Sorry, Howard," Billy said through gritted teeth, trying to pull himself up. "We'll pay for our stuff and get gone."

"Not you, Billy," Howard said, grasping Billy's hand, pulling him to his feet. "You and Malaya are more than welcome to take all the time you need. I'm talking to those two low-bred meth mouths." He glared at the Fleming brothers.

"Hell, I hate this dump anyways," Al said as he and Si sauntered toward the exit.

Billy thought they were sauntering pretty quickly. Probably had pockets full of packaged tooth rot and nose candy.

"I'm sorry about that," Howard said. "Those two weren't allowed in here already, but with the start of the month rush, I reckon no one saw 'em come in."

"That's okay," Billy said. "There's no fixing stupid. And I'm sorry about the mess. I'll help clean up." He tried to put weight on his right foot. Sucked air through his teeth as he nearly fell again.

"You get yourself on home, Billy," Howard said. "Get some ice on that knee. Better yet…"

Howard trotted down to the freezer cases, came back with a two pound bag of frozen store-brand peas.

"Here. On the house. Travis! Get over here, son!" Howard waved at a mountain-sized stock boy, a Deacons football shirt visible under his apron.

"Travis will help you out to your truck," Howard said. "Me and your missus will take care of the groceries. Keep those peas on your knee, you hear?"

"Thanks, Howard," Billy said as Travis pulled Billy's arm over his shoulders. "Been a long time since All-State baseball, hasn't it?"

Howard laughed, taking the buggy from Malaya and heading toward the checkout lanes.

"I'm a far better store manager than I ever was a shortstop. Get on home now. Me and Malaya will be out in no time."

Billy let Travis help him out to the truck. Well, "let" wasn't really the right word. No way he could've got there on his own without crutches.

They made it just as a deputy's brown car pulled up to the store's entrance.

"Aw, dang, Mr. Holbrook," Travis said. "That's a shitty thing for someone to do."

Someone, two guesses who, had gouged *Chink luver* into the truck's hood.

CHAPTER 4

BILLY AND MAL were silent on the way home. Malaya drove, the bench seat rucked so far forward that Billy's sore knee banged into the dash with every bump.

He clenched his teeth, biting back the cusses. Not Malaya's fault.

"I'm sorry about all that, Mal," he said when she finally shoved the shifter into park outside their home. "I should have done more."

Malaya hopped out, turned to look at him.

"Why sorry? Do you feel sorry when a dog does a poo? When a snake acts like a snake?"

"It's not like that. I'm your husband. I'm supposed to look out for you. Those two will keep on now, because they know I can't make them stop."

Malaya looked around the yard, at the house, at the bags of groceries in the truck bed.

"You take fine care of me," she said. "I am not bothered by monkeys. You should not be either. Monkeys jabber with no meaning. Monkeys like to throw their own poo. And monkeys will always be monkeys, whether or no you try to stop them. Now you sit. Wait. I bring your crutches."

She went inside, carrying more groceries than he'd have tried, bad knee or not, and came back a minute later with a pair of dusty aluminum crutches. The same crutches he had in their wedding portrait. Her bracelets pinged against the crutches, which were as tall as Malaya. Billy scowled.

"I hate these things," he groused, settling into them as he got out of the truck. Mal held the kitchen door for him as he hobbled toward the overstuffed blue couch in the living room.

Malaya went upstairs and came back with bottles of Zanaflex and Percocet, left over from before.

"You sit," she said, handing him one of each pill and a glass of water. "Peas on knees, please." She smiled down at him.

Billy laughed, in spite of the growing throbs in his knee. "Not bad, Mal. Not bad."

The pills made him foggy, and he dozed in and out until Malaya brought him a plate piled with noodles, shrimp, and gingered venison strips.

She sat in the armchair across from the couch, watching him eat, lamplight glinting off her silver bracelets.

Billy didn't much care for being stared at, but given how damn good everything tasted, he reckoned he could put up with a stare or two.

CHAPTER 5

THE NEXT DAY, Billy sanded down his old truck's hood and sprayed it with some primer. Ugly as hell, but at least those hateful words were gone.

His knee was killing him by the time he finished, shooting stabs of pain up and down his whole leg, even though he'd found the leg brace he'd worn for six weeks after he first hurt himself. Time to go sit and rest a while.

Inside, Malaya was up in her sewing room, a spare bedroom she'd taken over and filled with cloth, a treadle sewing machine, and an old Japanese *tansu* chest she'd brought with her from home. She'd also set up a small table where she kept all the statues and other stuff she'd brought with her.

Billy could hear her singing or chanting, but

couldn't make out the words, and didn't want to risk the short flight of steps up to the back room. So he got a Coke from the fridge and flopped down on the couch again. Time for another pain pill and muscle relaxer.

He was feeling some better, though. Shouldn't need the doctor this time.

He needed to decide what to do about the Fleming boys. He didn't want to worry about people being nasty to Malaya anytime they were in town, and the Flemings hadn't done anything he could call the sheriff about. Not yet, anyway.

He didn't have any proof they'd been the ones to scratch up his paint. Worse yet, Billy'd been the first one to act in the Pig. Al might be able to claim assault. No one would fault Billy, but still.

A lawyer would cost, and he didn't want to put Mal through all the courtroom nonsense.

Malaya came down before the pills kicked in. She brought him a steaming cup that smelled of cinnamon and ginger.

"You drink this," she said. "It will help you not to be sick from the medicine."

She knew how pukey opiates made him, bless her.

Besides, her teas always tasted great. Not like the bitter and foul brews his grandmother always mixed up.

"Thanks, Mal," he said before draining the cup. "You're the best."

He leaned back in the sofa as his eyelids drooped.

The last thing he saw was Malaya sitting in her armchair, her dark eyes focused on him.

CHAPTER 6

THE SOUND of tires crunching over gravel woke Billy. Malaya still sat across from him, but she looked to have changed clothes. Still her usual work shirt and dungarees, but fresh from the dryer or he'd eat his hat.

First things first. He needed a piss the way fish need water.

Billy groaned his way to his feet and stumbled to the john, scuffing his crutches on the floor, nearly falling with every step.

Them pills sure did make him sleep hard.

He did his business, then came back to the couch. He looked out the window, saw Sheriff Childress's brown Crown Vic outside. Must be about the fracas at the Piggly Wiggly. Not much else it could be.

Childress walked around Billy's truck, examining the fresh primer. Looked dry from here. Billy must've slept longer than he meant to.

He cracked the window and called out, "Come on in, Sheriff. Kitchen door's unlocked. I'm not walking too great right now."

The sheriff waved, then disappeared around the corner of the house. Malaya's gaze flicked toward the kitchen as the door opened, then closed. Childress came into view.

"How's the knee?" he said, taking off the hat that always put Billy in mind of a drill sergeant.

"Hurts like all get out. But I reckon I'll be fine in day or three. What can I do for you?"

"Judging from how your knee's puffed out from that brace, not a thing," Childress said. "I guess I should ask, just for form's sake. Where were you yesterday? Did you get out any?"

"You ought to know. Me and Mal puttered around the house until the afternoon, then we went out to town to do some shopping."

Sheriff Childress's eyebrows rose while Billy talked, threatening to join his hair.

"That was day before yesterday, Billy. I'm asking about *yesterday*."

"Day before?" What the hell? Pills must really have hit him hard. He took out his phone, saw the battery was almost flatline. Sure enough, he'd lost a whole day.

"I guess you're right," he said. "The Percocets

must get better with age. Why are you asking about yesterday?"

"Just following up any leads," Sheriff Childress said. "Just in case. I think it's probably a waste of time, all things considered. From what we can tell, yesterday afternoon, around two o'clock or so, Silas Fleming killed his brother Albert, then he managed to ride a spike into the great beyond. Overdosed. Heroin."

Billy's jaw dropped.

Malaya sat up a little straighter, still staring at Billy.

"What...I mean, how?" he said. "Why?"

"As to the *how*," the sheriff said, "looks like he split Al's head open with an axe. Or maybe a machete. Opened him up enough for what passed as his brains to leak out all over the place. As to the *why*, who knows? Maybe they got in a fight over their stash. Considering all the junk those two put in themselves day in and day out, Si might've thought Al was a giant purple people eater. He does the deed, then realizes what he's done, feels guilty, tries to kill the pain with a little too much horse and manages to kill himself instead."

"You think that's how it went down?" Billy's mouth was dry, but his palms were sweaty.

Malaya still stared at him.

"I think that's what'll sound best on my report," Childress said. "One neighbor said Si's Camaro wasn't there when Al got killed. I don't really care if those two did it to each other, or if some rivals took them out. The Fleming boys aren't any great loss to society, and whoever done for them probably had a good reason. Sorry I had to bother you folks, just needed to hear that you'd not been out and about yesterday."

Childress shook Billy's hand, tipped his hat to Malaya, and left.

Billy looked at his wife, who relaxed as the sheriff backed down the driveway.

"You need some food after your sleep." She stood, came over to him, kissed his cheek. "I have everything still to make more pancit palabok. You wait here, I will bring it to you."

"Thanks, Mal," Billy said, trying not to see the rusty red speckles on her silver bracelets. "You take good care of me. I love you, Malaya."

She gave him one of her rare smiles, then went to the kitchen to cook.

SWIFT'S

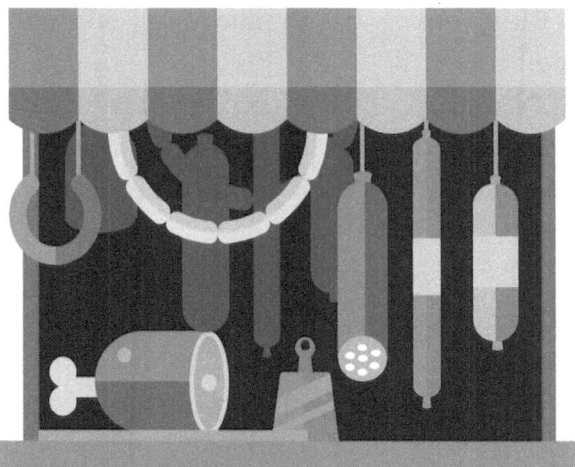

JASON A. ADAMS

For the foodies.

SWIFT'S

JULIE and I stroll down the aisles of Swift's Butcher Shop and Deli, checking out the latest offerings.

Swift's is a modest little place, kept open by government subsidies. Like all government-funded buildings, the interior is pretty drab. Dull green and white tile on the floor, bland beige walls, no décor to speak of. Just an industrial box with a door and windows.

But the counters and shelves... Those gleam under bright lights, the various meats spread in inviting displays. Red meat, white meat, sweetbreads. Everything to tempt a happy carnivore.

But the prepared dishes keep me coming back, more than the raw meats.

Swift's sells dishes from nearly every part of the world. Truly international cuisine. We buy supper from here nearly every single night.

A rack of tasty-looking tamales catches my eye, but I don't really feel like Mexican tonight. Julie oohs over some fresh Irish sausages, made from only the youngest stock and kept under dimmer lights so as not to darken the sensitive flesh. The next case holds Middle Eastern stews that smell heavenly.

Behind the counters, big burly guys in grey State Security uniforms with the Food Services Specialist emblem ply huge cleavers, dainty shears, long serrated knives; all the tools used to reduce the sides and quarters down to lunchmeat and steaks.

Julie motions to me, her lips moving, but I can't hear over a noisy bone saw. I go to her and immediately see why she wanted my attention.

This bin is full of fresh Indian. Biryani, curries, pandeeps. Yummity yum!

My stomach growls as I sample the vindaloo. Tender, moist, everything it should be. Vindaloo it is, along with some excellent German sauerbraten, a few lovely Irish sausages, and a token salad.

I wonder how the South Carolina bacon is today. That might make the perfect breakfast side tomorrow morning.

We head for the registers, our cart loaded with string-tied packages and takeout containers filled with coming pleasure. Julie is ahead of me, and I watch her hips sway as she walks. Curvaceous and toned. I sneak a tweak of her left cheek. Just right.

I'm glad she's been following my exercise and diet suggestions.

While a young girl in her ash-colored FS smock rings up our order, I reflect on how much things have changed since the Senate instituted the Food Services. Crime is down, poverty nearly gone, and hunger is only a bad memory. At least in this country. Not to mention how well the FS dealt with the refugee crisis.

Even Julie's family had benefitted, and I never thought her relatives would amount to anything. In the end, though, her sister and nephews amounted to $9.99 a pound.

I tweak Julie's rump again. I only need another few hundred bucks to make the down payment on the new Mercedes I've had my eye on, and she always says she wants to help me succeed in life.

I'm sure I'll miss her, but sometimes a man has to do his patriotic duty.

Even when his mouth is watering.

Birth of the Makmom

JASON A. ADAMS

For the Protectors of the world.

CHAPTER 1

ALL THAT HAS BEEN, will be again.

Thus had Brant of the *Makmorni*, the Sunset People, always believed. The idea was not new; it had been passed from grandfather to grandson since time out of mind.

Now Brant was the grandfather, only he had no grandsons to teach.

He sat on the still-frozen earth outside the hut of the Wise One, watching the clouds change into reddish-amber shapes as the sun went below the burial field's sacred mound on the shortest day of winter. The cold crept into his bones as he waited on Skala the Wise to summon him inside.

Overhead, the sacred oak tree spread its gigantic limbs protectively over Brant. Acrid smoke from the peat fires in the surrounding huts stung his eyes, but smelled of home and safety. All was peaceful and quiet, but he knew how quickly that could change.

Brant went over his weapons as he waited, an automatic habit. One he tried to impress upon the younger hunters and warriors. They listened to him, or at least most did. After all, did not the midsummer marks on his life-stone need all the fingers of five men to cover? A long life for a regular hunter, let alone for a warrior who bore scars and owned femurs from many upon many battles.

Brant's hair and beard still held some of the color of the evening clouds, but more and more the hairs drained and turned instead to something matching the dirty snow that still lay in the shade of the roundhouses.

Brant felt all of those summers, all of those gray hairs. He felt it in his bones and in his spirit. Life had been good, but he was tired.

The stone head of his war axe was loose. Brant took up a handful of the slushy snow, not feeling the cold in his work-hardened fingers and palm as he rubbed it into the sinew lashings until they were wet through. He used his teeth to pull the trailing end as he worked the ties, tasting the salty life force of the red deer who'd gifted the thongs to him by its death, tightening the oak haft against the heavy gray chert until he no longer felt any movement. He'd have to wait until the meeting with the Wise One ended and he got back to his own hearth to dry the cords, shrinking the lashings and tightening the weapon even further.

Only one weapon was allowed inside the hut of the Wise One. His grandfather's grandfather's war club.

Brant stood as Skala's withered face appeared at the roundhouse's opening. With the turf-covered walls and door framing her face, she looked a bit like a mossy turtle. With her white hair and whiter eyes, she might be more mound-spirit than turtle.

Brant did not smile at the thought, but it was not easy. Skala was not his grandmother, but they had always shared a relationship closer than most blood kin.

He ducked into the hut and squatted before the small turf fire at the center, looking up at Garm, his grandfather's grandfather.

His ancestor's skull peered down at him from its tiny platform of deer bone and auroch horn. The old man looked at him from behind those empty sockets as the light from the fire danced over his fleshless cheeks, and those of the smaller skull to his left. In the flickering light, both skulls took on that same red color. The color of the dusklit clouds, of Brant's hair, of the lumps embedded in the huge war club propped against the platform.

Garm's club was a weapon suited to the man's

legend. Nearly as tall as Brant, nearly as thick as his wrist. Studded with unique chunks of not-stone.

Those lumps were unlike anything Brant had ever seen anywhere else. In the entire clan, or of the clans as far as Brant had traveled, nearly thirty day's fast walking, no one knew of what they were made.

Each smooth nodule was the size of his large toe. They held some sort of magic, for they would slowly turn green throughout the season, until they resembled the flesh of a dead man right before it falls from the bones. Once every year, on the night of the midwinter festival, the lumps were rubbed with oil-soaked leather until the green vanished and they shone forth as though they were captured drops of the evening sun.

The smaller skull above would look down at the restoration, and if it deemed work and worker worthy, would restore the power of the sun so the crops and animals could grow, the babies quicken, the clan thrive.

Garm would look on, protecting his charge in death as he had in life.

Garm's companion served as the clan's totem and god. In life, he had been *Donkeek't*, The Saving Hand. The name was not easy. It came from some other language, perhaps not one spoken by natural men.

Legend held that Donkeek't had driven the B'zuni—another tongue-bending name—from the land, saving the Makmorni and all the other clans from destruction. Donkeek't had fallen in the battle, slain as he finished the final magic to bind the B'zuni from the land.

Garm had given his life protecting Donkeek't long enough to work his spell.

Brant had asked his grandfather about the B'zuni, but the old man knew little. He had not yet been born when Garm fell.

"Creatures of fog and smoke," he had told the wide-eyed youngster. "Black as a cloudy night. Cold as the water that kills. Devoid of kindness. Full of hate."

"Where do they come from?" Brant had asked.

"*Elsewhere,*" his grandfather replied in a low whisper. "Outside. Between the shadow and the earth, maybe. They are not of this world, boy. Yet they hate this world and everything in it. Were it not for Donkeek't, there would no longer *be* a world."

Brant joined Skala in the midwinter chanting, polishing the ancient war club until the embedded lumps shone bright in the firelight.

Above him, Garm and Donkeek't smiled down on Brant and Skala.

CHAPTER 2

BIRDSONG FILLED the air as Brant once again walked to the hut of the Wise One. Mud squelched around his leather-shod feet, still chilly although no ice remained. The warm sun eased the ache in his right shoulder, calling forth a smile from beneath his graying whiskers. The dark clouds swelling to the east told him to enjoy the warmth while he may. Even now, a cool breeze stirred the leaves and set loose skins flapping.

Skala sat before the hut's sacred fire, staring up at Garm and his companion. She did not speak as Brant entered, and he saw the wide eyes and slack face that spoke of an ergot-fueled journey inward.

"Greetings, Skala," he said, sitting down on the other side of the hearth, where her eyes, and hopefully her spirit, would see him.

"Shadows," she whispered, her voice quavery

and indistinct. "Banes. Terror upon the land. They come…they come…you must protect…"

Skala's white hair fell around her face as her chin drooped. Her blind gaze still remained on the two totems above, eyes straining upward even as her head lowered.

"What comes?" Brant asked. "What perils approach? Speak, O Skala. Tell me what the spirits show you."

Now the old woman began to slowly rock to and fro, bony arms wrapped tightly about herself, yellowed fingernails digging into her thin shoulders. Tears leaked from her unseeing eyes, carving tracks down her soot-stained cheeks.

"All we know will end," she said, voice cracking and breath catching. "Nothing will stop that. If you fail, Brant, grandson of Garm's grandson, the child will die too soon and the world will join him."

A chill ran down Brant's entire body, raising bumps on his flesh and the hair on his neck.

"For the Makmorni, there is nothing," Skala said, voice deepening and strengthening with resolve. "But for you and for Donkeek't, there is yet hope. And as your fortunes rise and fall, so too the fortunes of all living things. They—"

Skala's intonation broke off as shudders wracked her thin frame. She stiffened, face drawing in pain, then toppled slowly sideways. Brant watched her chest heave shakily once, twice, then no more.

"Skala?" he asked, his voice little more than a babe's sigh.

No answer.

"Skala." he said, more loudly now.

Nothing.

Brant got to his feet, knees popping like pine knots in a fire. He went to Skala's side, shaking her gently, then more roughly.

"Skala!" he yelled. "Stay! I need to know—"

Skala's body jerked and convulsed. Her eyelids fluttered and she moaned.

That moan chilled Brant's blood. It came from far beyond her old body, from below and between the solid places of the world.

Finally, she blinked, coughed, and sat up.

"Brant," she said. "Did you hear?"

"Yes, Wise One," he said. "I heard. But I do not understand."

"You will, Brant of the Makmorni," she said, gazing upon him with sadness and resignation in her blank white eyes. "All too well."

CHAPTER 3

BRANT LEFT THE HUT, meaning to find some hot broth for Skala. The breeze had become a wind, blowing grit into his face, making him squint and cough.

The folk of his clan dashed hither and yon, gathering baskets, skins, and other light items that danced in the growing gale. Shadows trembled in the failing light as the clouds engulfed the sun, sending the temperature downward and throwing the village into semi-darkness.

Brant stopped in his tracks, trying to blink the dust from his eyes.

The entire sky was filled with clouds. The sun no longer shone down.

Yet the shadows continued to walk.

He stood thunderstruck as one of the shadows sprouted huge bat-like wings, enfolding Teela, a young girl only a month from her womanhood rites. She screamed, thin and reedy, her voice muffled far more than the wind noise could account for.

The shadow released her and she fell, blue and lifeless.

The nearest Makmorni gaped at her dead body, looking this way and that for the cause, passing right over the swarming shadow beasts.

The voice of Brant's grandfather rang in his mind.

"Creatures of fog and smoke," he muttered to himself.

The B'zuni had returned.

More shrieks sounded throughout the collection of huts as the shadows embraced the villagers, leaving death behind. Brant snatched up his war axe from beside the entry to the Wise One's hut and he ran toward the nearest, yelling his war cry, swinging the heavy polished stone blade toward where the B'zuni's head should be.

The ululating cry died on his lips as the axe swept through the being with no resistance, and no effect.

The B'zuni turned toward Brant, wings unfurling in a slow, almost lazy motion. Brant braced himself and raised his useless axe. His time had come, but he'd not go down cowering. He would fight to the end.

From the branches of the sacred oak burst a

hissing, spitting creature in a whirlwind of fur the color of sunset clouds. It tore into the B'zuni's head clawing and biting until streams of tarry ichor flew threw the air. The B'zuni emitted a head-piercing keen which Brant felt more than heard. And then it faded into the night, and its attacker landed on the ground, growling deep in its throat and looking for another target.

It was one of the great lynxes that dwelt alongside the Makmorni. One of that animal tribe which were the only creatures held taboo to hunt or harm since long before the telling of stories.

Behind him, Skala cried out.

"Brant! Take this!"

He turned and caught the object Skala threw at him. It was Garm's war club. Brant's palms tingled with…something, and he felt new energy course through his elderly frame.

Brant whirled and swung the mighty weapon at the nearest B'zuni with all his force.

Instead of passing through as his axe had done, the club smashed into the thing with the popping sound of a burst apple. A bright flash stung his eyes, and the creature exploded into tendrils of smoke that dissipated quickly in the rising gale.

Around the village, more furry bodies flung themselves against the B'zuni, screeching their own battle cries and shredding the insubstantial creatures.

Brant raced through the huts, swinging Garm's club, striking down shadows left and right. Before he realized it, he was out of the ring of dwellings and into the forest.

To his rear, the battle between lynx and B'zuni raged, although he could hear more of the wildcats than the shadows.

Turning to rejoin the fray, Brant nearly tripped over a bundle at the foot of another great oak tree. He started to step over the pile of fur and skins, until it moved.

Brant froze, but the pile was of hides no longer attached to their owners. He reached down to toss it aside, and saw a small face.

A boychild's face.

Had one of the village women fled to the forest with her child, and then dropped it?

Brant scooped the boy up and ran back to the hut of the Wise One. Skala could watch the babe until all was safe again.

He was still many body-lengths from the hut when a swarm of B'zuni shook off their feline harassers and swooped through the air toward him.

Clutching the child in his left arm, Brant raised the heavy club in his right, bracing his feet.

The child reached out its chubby pink hand and touched Brant's wrist with two fingers.

Cold ripped through Brant. Not the dead chill of

the B'zuni, but rather the pure cold of clear snow, new ice.

A blinding silver flash shot forth from every embedded not-stone in Garm's club, rays spearing out and skewering the B'zuni between him and Skala, burning images of exploding shadows onto the back of his eyes.

Brant ran toward Skala again, bright spots hiding her tent even as his feet carried him unerringly to the low opening. He thrust the child into her arms, then turned and ran back to the fight.

Time passed as Brant swung Garm's club, destroying shadows with every blow. The lynx pack brought down nearly as many, although far too great a number of their golden-furred bodies lay strewn across the village.

Finally, the remaining B'zuni melted away, slipping under rocks, behind trees, into the dark places. Brant leaned on his club, panting with his efforts.

But not sore, save for the places where icy claws had drawn burning lines on his arms and back. In fact, although exhausted, he felt better than he had in many summers.

CHAPTER 4

HE WENT TO SKALA THEN, ducking into her hut. He hoped she would have the wisdom of all this.

Skala sat once again before the central hearth. Beside her, the still bundled child lay upon a bed of rushes and soft heather. His head was propped on a peat pillow. Hair blacker than the darkest night framed a face as pale as milk. Two eyes the color of new leaves looked into Brant's own, with an intelligence that bothered the big man.

"Sit, Warrior," Skala said. "We must speak of many things."

"Were those the B'zuni of legend?" Brant asked, squatting on the other side of the fire, finishing the ritual triangle with Skala and the boy.

"I believe so," she said. "Tell me, O Brant, what appearance had they?"

"They looked like men made of the oil smoke

that comes from burning flesh," Brant said. "But with the wings of bats. They flew and flowed like no bird or bat, though."

"That agrees with what my mind's eye beheld," the old woman said. "Could the others see them?"

"I do not know. I don't understand, but the people looked through and past them, as though blind to their presence."

Skala drew a deep breath, the lines on her seamed face deepening, then let it out slowly, cheeks puffing.

"And so it begins again," she said. "Did the child touch you at all?"

"Yes, he touched my wrist, and light went through my body and out of Garm's stick."

"Not Garm's," she said, patting his hand as she smiled sadly up at him.

"*Your* stick. I have watched and waited many and many summers for this."

Skala gathered the babe and placed him in Brant's arms.

"Do you not recognize this child, O Brant?"

Brant stared into the babe's pale face, into eyes far too old for the body that held them. Then he looked up at the two skulls in their place of honor.

"Yes," Skala said. "We no longer have need of those old bones. Our living totems have come again."

In his arms, the child smiled serenely.

"Is this...is he..." Brant stammered, unable to finish the thought.

"Yes, my poor Brant. The Donkeek't has returned. And he must have a protector to shield him while he does what he must. You are descended of Garm's line. You can see the shadows, and you can channel the Donkeek't's power."

Skala took the child back, laid him in his bed, took both of Brant's massive hands in her small, withered fingers.

"You, Brant. You are the one I have watched for. Waited for. Even more than for the Donkeek't. I knew he would come someday, and that I would know him when I felt him. *You* were the one I was unsure of."

She raised his hands to her lips, kissed them tenderly, then raised her face to his again.

"You have a great burden ahead of you, O Brant, but you must accept it freely. The Donkeek't must have his protector, as I have said. Garm was that protector when last the Donkeek't lived among us, but he died as the Donkeek't's previous body did."

Brant looked upon the skull of his forbearer, and the empty bones of the Donkeek't's previous vessel. His head seemed too full, too many strange things causing his thoughts to tangle against one another.

Skala looked at the relics not at all.

"Will you take his place, O Brant? Will you fulfill your destiny?"

Brant rocked back on his haunches, gaze darting between his ancient teacher and this strange infant. He had always been a protector of the clan, watching over his people whenever wild beasts or wilder strangers threatened.

"I am old, Skala," he finally said. "Not the man I once was."

"You are not today as old as you were yesterday, Brant."

"I don't know what you mean," Brant said, hoping he was right.

"Ah, but you do," said the Wise One. She groped forward, gently tugged a lock of his hair.

"Tell me, my protector. Did the battle age you?"

Brant stared, jaw hanging. The lock of hair still held some frost, but most of the red of his youth had returned. As he saw this, he noticed that his bad shoulder no longer ached, even though the club was heavy and he'd wielded it long. He swallowed hard.

"Are you certain this is the Saving Hand?" Brant was no seer, no holy man. Why would the Hand come to him, instead of to another?

Outside the hut, a low rumble grew. Brant felt no fear at the noise. It was not the rumble of stones or storm, rather he felt peace somehow.

Skala's smile held mirth now, instead of sadness.

"Take the child outside," she said. "Hold his hand in yours and do what comes to you."

He took the babe up again, felt a tiny fist close around his index finger. Gasped when he stepped from the hut.

A ring of orange and gray lynxes surrounded the roundhouse, giving voice to soft rumbles of pleasure which grew louder when they saw what Brant held. Many of them bled from flesh rent by shadowy talons.

One of the great cats lay before the door, leaking scarlet into the mud from a long gash in its belly. Its yellow eyes were closed, its breath ragged.

With his free hand, Brant stroked its fur, marveling at the softness of such a fearsome fighter.

Again that eerie power flowed through Brant's body. Starting where the child, the Saving Hand, held his finger. Across his chest, down his arm, through his hand and into the dying cat.

Where Brant stroked, the long cut began to seal. In moments, the lynx opened its eyes, stood and shook itself. Then it fell in beside Brant as he moved along the circle, stroking each of the purring wildcats in turn until all were made whole.

CHAPTER 5

LATE THAT EVENING, as the Makmorni keened the dead and prepared the bodies for their final journey, Brant once again sat with Skala and the Donkeek't, flanked by the mighty lynx he—they—had cured, and a female with nearly identical markings.

"Have you chosen?" Skala asked, spooning porridge into the child's mouth.

"There is no choice to be made," Brant said. "I am sworn to defend our people, and this child, the Donkeek't, is one of us by the fire of battle."

"I am glad to hear it," the Wise One said. "Then you pledge your life to his protection? To guard and shield him whenever the need arises, until your own death frees you?"

"I do pledge," Brant said, laying his palm on the Donkeek't's brow. "So long as my heart beats, so long as I breathe."

Another of those surges coursed through him, powerful enough that Skala felt it where she sat under the two skulls. The tufts on the cats' ears flattened as though in a wind, and the purring swelled.

Skala and the child smiled up at Brant, even as they wept.

"I am proud of you, my protector," said Skala through her tears. "And so very, very sorry, for your life will indeed be long."

"Is long life a thing to weep for?"

"I'm afraid only you will be able to answer that, in time," she said. "You will live, and you will fight, and you will mourn. But, when fate permits, you will also have the gift of forgetting. For a time, at least."

Over the millennia to come, Brant would learn the truth of Skala's prophecy and curse himself for a fool, even as he took up arms over and over again, honoring the vow he grew to hate.

Thank you for joining us on these adventures!

Explore more from Jason's Brain Squirrel Garden at
www.JasonAdamsBooks.com

ALSO BY JASON A. ADAMS

I hope you enjoyed reading the stories in *Tales from the Squirrel Garden* as much as I enjoyed writing them.

Visit www.jasonadams.info and join the adventure for exclusive new fiction, my past and future travels, and whatever else strikes my fancy. Hope to see you there!

Novellas:

Agonist

Collections and Anthologies:

Normally Fantastic

On the Case!

Capeless Heroes

Through the Squirrel Tree

(with Kari Kilgore)

Partnership in Crime

Shadows Mountain Deep

Partners in Romance

Near Future Forward

ABOUT JASON

Jason A. Adams writes across the spectrum. His stories include science fiction, fantasy, horror, Appalachian folk tales, and romance, of course.

You can find more of his work at www.JasonAdamsBooks.com.

Jason's stories also appear in several issues of *Pulphouse Magazine, Mystery, Crime, and Mayhem, Uncollected Anthology, Thrill Ride,* and WMG Publishing's Holiday Spectaculars.

Jason, a recovering Air Force brat who grew up all over the US and Japan, now perches in the mountains of Southwest Virginia with his excellent author wife Kari Kilgore (www.karikilgore.com), several spoiled-rotten house critters, and assorted wild visitors from the nearby forest.

news@JasonAdamsBooks.com

 facebook.com/Jason.A.Adams.2

ADDITIONAL COPYRIGHT INFORMATION

Cupids

To Catch a Thief

Print ISBN-13: 979-8-62-033547-3